D0021380

Also by Viken Berberian

The Cyclist: A Novel

Das Kapital

A novel of love and money markets

Viken Berberian

Simon & Schuster
NEW YORK LONDON TORONTO SYDNEY

SIMON & SCHUSTER
Rockefeller Center
1230 Avenue of the Americas
New York, NY 10020

Manufactured in the United States of America

10 9 8 7 6 5 4 3 2 1

Library of Congress Cataloging-in-Publication Data
Berberian, Viken.
Das kapital : a novel of love and money markets / Viken Berberian.
p. cm.
1. Wall Street (New York, N.Y.)—Fiction. 2. Investment advisors—Fiction. I. Title.

PS3602.E75D37 2007
813'.6—dc22

2007011726

For information regarding special discounts for bulk purchases, please contact Simon & Schuster Special Sales at 1-800-456-6798 or business@simonandschuster.com.

ISBN-13: 978-0-7432-6723-6
ISBN-10: 0-7432-6723-0

For Sako, Lorig, Ara and Alix of Sahel

On the following day, when fuller reports came in, the market began to slide off, but even then not as violently as it should. Knowing that nothing under the sun could stave off a substantial break I doubled up and sold five thousand shares. . . . I wasn't plunging recklessly. I was really playing conservatively. There was nothing that anyone could do to undo the earthquake, was there? They couldn't restore the crumpled buildings overnight, free, gratis, for nothing, could they? All the money in the world couldn't help much in the next few hours, could it? . . .

—EDWIN LEFÈVRE, *REMINISCENCES OF A STOCK OPERATOR*

Gravitation is not responsible for people *falling* in love.

—ALBERT EINSTEIN

Das Kapital

1.

HE DREAMT THAT THE WORLD was coming to an end. Yet he knew that this was a dream and not a nightmare. There was no sign of a tumultuous ending, of the sky falling down. There were no screams or sirens. He sat in front of a computer screen, Zenlike, watching the numbers fall. He could tell by the size of their drop that something terrible had happened. He did not have to listen to the news to know this. The numbers said everything. He went deeper into sleep, resigned to an inner faintness. He rolled over in his bed, an oracular smile on his face, as if he had known all of this would somehow happen.

He let out a laugh as one benchmark tumbled after another. Then someone whispered in his ear: "Shshhhhhhhh. Sell, Wayne, sell, or you'll be wiped out. Shshhhhhhhh. Sell, Wayne, sell, you better sell now."

He pressed a few more keys, like a concert pianist playing a mournful prelude, an end-of-the-world elegy to humanity. An amber graph appeared on the upper left-hand corner of his screen, charting the big bang of the human heart. Then, without warning, the numbers halted their fall. A searing pain penetrated his lumbering body.

When he woke up, everything around him was just as it had been the day before.

His loft was functional, almost empty. There were the requisite designer pieces: the pliable plastic bookcase inspired more by itself than by the ideas that it held; the hand-woven *tatami* in place of a back-friendly mattress; the Ingo Maurer lamp whose fragile frame suggested a home absent of children. The floor was cement gray, just as it had been yesterday. He looked out his windows across the West Side Highway. The abandoned warehouses were still there, remnants of a forgotten recession when he was still a toddler.

There was order all around him. His undershirts were stacked by increments of seven. His books were arranged by color. His furniture was mostly Nordic, linear. He woke up at five every morning, including Sundays, not because he was an insomniac, but because there was work to be done. He checked the weather forecast along the Mediterranean basin, measured the tropics of terror below the thirty-fifth parallel; the corn yield in Kansas; the price of Brent Crude oil at $50 a barrel; the cases of missing forests, wholly uprooted, whittled and wasted, unreported.

Nature. He disliked its prickly stems, its bramble and bush, the obstinate precision of its cycles, its preconfigured calendar, the coded tapestry of its patterns, the singular and undeviating smugness of its hills, standing stubbornly in the way of human progress.

Before going to work he studied the atlas under a desk lamp, passing his magnifying glass over deltas, oceans and valleys. From Kabul to New York, always drifting from the periphery to the core, in precise concentric circles. At the office he stared into a luminous screen, into his precipitous and fateful future. He was chained to his Bloomberg. And yet to him, the *Gloomberg,* as he sometimes called the news retrieval system perched on his desk, was more than a processor of bad news. It was a repository of the *outside* world; a guardian of numerical itineraries; a facilitator of greater wealth and its destruction.

In the financial community he is simply known as Wayne. There have been unconfirmed sightings at the Odeon, where someone claims to have seen him once eating with his hands, even of pissing on his plate. They are not to be believed. Rumors. They are there to be denied, or if the market is open, to be traded on.

At the Midtown offices of the hedge fund a heavy downpour drummed on the windows. Then, all of a sudden, the rain stopped and a streak of sunlight broke through a cumulus cloud. Wayne looked outside. The surrounding landscape was a concentration of glass and steel, vertical gulags lost in the clouds below. Facing his electronic terminal, he felt like he was in the cockpit of a fighter jet, a creature of pure movement and speed. Trading was like space-time arbitrage, the twisting vectors of a supersonic jet. It did not matter whose side he was on. He belonged to a society where transactions superseded human relations. There were no friends or enemies in the steel and glass towers, just transactions, best made in silence or against the neutral whir of the air conditioner.

He looked into the Bloomberg. Everything became clear again. There were familiar diagrams on his two screens. Each plotted point was the expression of a just measure. Each fraction was a clue to a hidden treasure. Each decimal lent dignity to a perverse pleasure, until a 24K bloc crossed the tape. The bids were relentless, growing bigger in size. This made Wayne neither happy nor sad. He took pride in dominating the odds, but when they turned against him, he rarely complained, pretending to be immune to the market's gyrations, to the occasional dirty tricks that life played on him.

"It's a hostile takeover," his trader said.

"How's it being financed?"

"Not sure yet, just hit the tape. Let me call some guys and get a refresher on it."

"Forget it, just lose it. Let's just fucking get out."

He felt triumphant at the end of the third calendar quarter.

Most hedge funds had lost money betting on a rebound. Screw them. He had warned them of the coming catastrophe, but they did not listen. Now they would have to pay with their lives. Whose fault was that? Last week he warned a portfolio manager about buying shares of Mickey Ds. "Dude, everyone likes a hamburger," the manager shot back. "It's like a noncyclical stock. I don't know what the right price is, but if it goes up, God Bless America."

"But it's not gonna go up," Wayne said. "It has no juice."

"Trust me, it's gonna rip."

"Rip, my ass. It's sitting on its ass."

"Whatever, dude."

Wayne turned his attention to another beleaguered stock. He entered the ticker of a Corsican timber company into the Bloomberg. The Bustaci Frères Fibre Company was the only papermaker in the world located on an island. Most of the traders who bought and sold Bustaci stock did not know that Corsica was an island, or that it was the birthplace of Napoleon, or that the Corsicans spoke their own language, which was perhaps not as cryptic as Armenian but was quite difficult to discern in its own right. All they cared about was whether Bustaci would produce more timber next year than last, or if it would increase its output of corrugated cardboard, or if the stock price went up or down. On the global exchanges investors took a bulimic stance on Bustaci shares and their bouts of irrational buying were often followed by episodes of self-induced vomiting. No one knew the reason for this obsessive behavior. The stock made an effort to climb back at the start of the week following a Lehman Brothers upgrade.

"I've spoken with the Lehman analyst," Wayne shouted to no one in particular. "This is one brother who has his head up his ass."

"It's up a buck," his trader IM'd back.

"It's a fake-out, sell more of it."

"You got it, boss."

A few minutes later the stock began to drop just as Wayne had surmised.

"I knew I was right," Wayne said. "This bitch is going down faster than a Ukrainian hooker."

And so he sat in front of his Bloomberg, frozen, watching the numbers fall, as if the world were coming to a quiet, civilized end. If history was any guide, no one knew what would happen next. "Sell, sell, sell," Wayne screamed at his Bloomberg. "Sell, or you'll be wiped out!" Soon after this visceral outburst the S&P faltered and one benchmark tumbled after another. Nasdaq dropped the most since the bombings in Beirut. At the end of June, the S&P dropped twelve handles. Wayne instructed the trade desk to raise cash and prepare for a sharper fall.

When the market closed he looked at the plants next to his desk. They looked more uncertain than the stock symbols on his screen. He ran his palm over a leaf. It felt like an extraterrestrial tongue, viscous and velvety. This sensation made him twitch, this feeling of being affected by an alien world. He longed for something familiar, like the comforting pattern of an oblong distribution. He felt a little guilty about this. Was the idea of an oblong-shaped leaf any less credible than an ordinary one? He examined the plant, but this time he did not see green. He began to count the recurring patterns in the leaves. There were five main lobes radiating from the stem. The sublobes were similar to the larger ones in outline, structured in overlapping spirals. They were arranged in a logarithmic Fibonacci sequence:* 1, 1, 2, 3, 5, 8, 13, 21, 34, 55, and so on and so on. He felt at peace counting the numbers, over and over again. It was music to his ears, a paean to phi (ø), which was the closest he ever hoped to get to perfection.

2.

THE ONLY NUMBERS that the Corsican counted were those of trees. He counted them as he hiked through the island's glorious forests. Unlike Wayne, he considered a tree just a tree; a

* The ratios of successive Fibonacci numbers approach the golden ratio as *n* approaches infinity.

fern was a fern, an arbutus was an arbutus and forests were full of all kinds of herbs and a great many bushes, and never in his life had he encountered a leaf with an oblong distribution. If he knew that they existed he'd have done his best to avoid them. Nor did the Corsican care much for Fibonacci, especially during such a bright, beautiful day. A pie was something one ate, nothing worth losing one's hair over.

The Corsican felt especially ebullient today. Nature was everywhere around him, ascendant. Tiny star-shaped flowers covered the valley in pink. He picked one and patiently chewed its bulb, just as his ancestors had: a piece of the prehistoric past interpolated into the present. He opened his sack and filled it with the ambrosial buds to offer to his commanders. Grown men with delicate hearts, they too were prepared to kill in defense of the pink flower.

Walking through a field, he could see the roots of history laid bare in crystallized, elemental forms. The clouds were in retreat, needled by beams of sunlight, and tiny petrels flitted over the foliage in the mountainous interior of the island. When he emerged from the maquis he could see the ancient city of Corte perched on top of a hill. As he entered the city, many people came to see him. They shook his hand and showered him with flowers. The children ran around him in circles. A young girl approached him and kissed his hand as if he were a king or a prophet. The Corsican continued his walk up a winding path at the top of which was a fortress. It was surrounded on all sides by primordial rock. His commanders were huddled in a stony barrack, waiting for him, or rather, for the news that he carried. But he kept them waiting. The air smelled of moss, a lingering antediluvian past, though it also smelled of *brocciu,* ewe's cheese, and chestnut flour pastry. Some of them were busy finishing up breakfast when the Corsican walked in and offered them the pink flowers. They tore the delicate petals and began to chew on them. This cacophonous communion was fraught with such emotion that one of the commanders almost cried. As the chewing subsided, the Corsican surveyed the commanders with his strange, protuberant eyes. He was the human reincarnation of a sublime species of fish, condemned by some supernatural power to live among ordinary men. The commanders waited for him to break the silence. When he finally opened his mouth, he knew that it was nature speaking, this colossal crashing of a wave unhinged from its center of gravity. He looked at his watch. The commanders anxiously waited for news from that other island, where nature was a Hobbesian jungle of computer screens ordered inside black geometric towers.

"I leave for New York City tomorrow," the Corsican said. "I am supposed to meet him inside the MetLife Building, that icon of capitalism condensed; beacon of betrayal to us, symbol of prosperity to them."

Two days later the Corsican was in a city cab, watching his driver eat from a paper bucket made by Bustaci. It contained a plastic fork and last night's takeout of General Tso's chicken.

"Don't mind me eating," the cabdriver said. "I skipped breakfast this morning."

So had the Corsican. The food they served on the plane had made him nauseous. When the cab crawled to a stop at Fifty-seventh and Madison his stomach rumbled. Then the sky thundered. Clouds converged. Umbrellas emerged. An ominous pall fell over Midtown Manhattan.

"Tempu catt ìu," the Corsican said. Bad weather. "I am not going to make it on time."

"As always, time and money are the problems," the driver tried to console him. "When I was a professor at the New School I always liked to talk about Marx to my students and I permitted myself to become homiletic."

The Corsican nodded. It was the little affirmation that the driver needed: "I tell my young passengers the same thing today. That because they're young and relatively privileged, they don't understand the fundamental truth Marx grasped early and chose to grasp as a tragedy. We sell the time of our lives for wages. It's not just that time is money. It's that life, which is energy exercised over time, is exchanged for money. Life is money; energy is money; time is money. Money is the universal solvent, which brings us to the MetLife Building, your destination, or, more likely, another point of departure. That'll be forty dollars."

The Corsican gave the driver two twenty-dollar bills and stepped into a mass of flesh: elbows jostling elbows; agitated crowds swelling at street corners; buildings spitting out humans in some kind of an inventory-purging event; a man eating a wet hot dog while walking in the rain. Towering over Midtown Manhattan was the MetLife Building, where Wayne sat behind his desk, screaming into a next-generation handheld:

"Hey, brain fart, listen to me for a second. Just buy the fucking ten-year. Trust me on this, it's gonna rip." Minutes later the Friday payroll report sparked a sell-off in equities. The economy added fewer jobs than everyone expected. Bonds surged. "Bad news is good news," Wayne said to his screens and to no one else in particular. "Everyone is pukin' out stocks and buying Treasuries."

The Corsican made his way through a thick crowd, wrestling with umbrellas that looked bigger than any he had seen. He was nearly run over by a cab as he crossed an intersection. By the time he approached the building he was soaking. He took the elevator to the thirty-first floor, where an intern from Empiricus Kapital greeted him. He walked past a poster by Rothko glorifying the Industrial Revolution: a man holding a giant hammer in one hand and a bouquet of red tulips in the other.

The Corsican walked around Empiricus, surveying the overeducated team of knowledge workers. Most of them had the look of institutional boredom etched in their faces. They sat behind wafer-thin screens, tracking the undulations of the market, trying to make sense of its volatility, its sudden surges and kinetic crashes. He looked closely into their fallow eyes. Their source of life seemed to come from outside, from the artificial glow of the filtered neon lighting. Most of the staff could be found in the trading pit, sitting behind industrial desks, their eyes glued to flickering screens. There were no partitions at Empiricus. The physical organization of the office was anti-hierarchical by nature, so that on first appearance it was not clear who was actually running the place. Behind Wayne's desk on the wall was a poster with a reworked quotation from Karl Marx in big bold letters:

> *We have drowned the most heavenly ecstasies of religious fervor, of chivalrous enthusiasm, of philistine sentimentalism, in the icy water of egotistical calculation. We have resolved personal worth into exchange value, and in the face of the numberless indefeasible freedoms, have set up that single, all-consuming freedom, free trade.*

It was an odd epigram to have in an investment firm, but everything about this office was unusual. Next to Wayne sat the fund's chief research analyst, Pintu Banerjee, credited for developing an anticipatory inflation gauge. Wayne rarely made a bet on disaster without consulting Banerjee. The Bengali was an expert in the esoteric field of Indian bonds and stochastic volatility, which became the blueprint of a trade Wayne engineered against the rupee. Banerjee lit a Four Square cigarette and inhaled deeply, knowing full well that lung cancer strikes one in three of the smoker population. It was difficult to tell why Banerjee, for whom risk aversion was extreme, smoked so heavily. In the financial community, at least, he longed for longevity. He took another puff, by his last count his sixty-seventh of the day. He smoked in quick succession and with a particular kind of listlessness. He was grateful that Wayne tolerated his smoking.

Banerjee took a break from the keyboard and measured the Corsican as he walked past him. He quickly ascribed to him a mental zero. He then examined the green square on his cigarette box and was reminded of home. The logo was designed by Satyaji Raj, the Bengali filmmaker, all of whose movies he had seen. With each puff he dreamt of his alternate history as a Bollywood scriptwriter.

The Corsican sensed a concentrated field of energy around Banerjee's two screens as he walked past the smoke-engulfed Bengali. Advancing columns of amber-colored integers filled his screens. He caught a glimpse of an unintelligible formula through the fumes. There was an irrational root and a three-dimensional triangle embedded inside.

Next to the Bengali was Simone Cordoba, chief currency trader at Empiricus Kapital. She was half Swiss, half Argentine, daughter of the Harvard-educated Armando Cordoba, former deputy finance minister of Argentina, in charge of currency devaluation and wholesale national impoverishment. When during her interview Wayne criticized her father's policies, she hardly flinched:

"I'm sure you know that Wall Street benefited immensely from my father's devaluation policy," she said. "It was 1986 and the Argentineans soon lost the euphoria of winning the World Cup. Then an offshore hedge fund attacked our currency."

"Their net exposure was nominal," Wayne interjected. "It wasn't who you think it was."

"I'm not being critical or defensive, just making a point."

"Hedge funds are an interesting dynamic, for sure, but we're never the driver in that sort of thing. What I'm getting at is that we'd love to hire your dad as a consultant."

That's when Wayne decided to hire Simone Cordoba. It had nothing to do with the size of her breasts, which her stretch-knit chiffon blouse made even more salient. For anyone who might think that Wayne is a sexist, that's a moot point open to debate, but let it be noted for the record that at the time he decided to hire Simone Cordoba his mind was charting the shape of the Treasury yield curve and nothing else.

Next to Cordoba sat Dr. Wang, who was busy writing a quarterly client report titled "D Is for Destruction." He had small, intelligent eyes and politically correct nipples and he wrote his reports while listening to Mahler. What a bunch of inspired guys, the Corsican thought. I can't wait not to see them again. When he finally reached Wayne he was yelling into the phone, "This trade is pretty good, but you should be ten times bigger in it. Not *two* times, *ten* times. There's no way it's gonna fail. The *vol* on this bitch is gonna explode. We'll cover four, five points lower."

Wayne was in his late twenties, talking to traders twice his age. At twenty-eight, the Corsican had still been spray-painting national liberation slogans on granite cliffs: *libertà per tutti patriotti.* If one day he decided to have a city job he would have to literally reinvent his résumé. For what could he claim as professional experience? Listening to the rustling of leaves, pilfering of hens, collecting seashells. If truth be told, he had some experience ravaging forests, for until recently he had worked for the Bustaci Frères Fibre Company.

As he grew used to the devastation around him he felt anger at his predicament and so one day he made a secret pact with nature to restore its honor. His other secret wish was to be fired, for he also felt shame at his profession. With each swing of the axe he chipped away at his beliefs and sometimes at the end of the day his body convulsed from the shock of the mechanized pogroms he and his friends committed against nature, more violent than the massacre of the Algerians, for whom he felt contempt, and he would raise his head enraged and let out a Munch-like scream filled with pain and horror. He had a special talent for identifying trees. His favorite was the tough maritime pine called the laricio. He respected the laricio more than any other tree and never approached it with an axe. To strike one down would have been more shameful than to marry an Arab. He was not a racist. Nor did he harbor any ill sentiment against the Arabs who lived in Bastia on the eastern shore of the island; he just wanted a Corsica for the Corsicans. It was not the Algerians' fault that he was fired from his job. The Arabs were not the ones selling shares of Bustaci. How many Arab day traders were there with names like Lenny, Itzak and Wayne? He did not know of any. He was just proud to be Corsican. One day he would marry one. If someone asked him whether he was French or Corsican his response depended on who was asking. If the person was French he would tell him he was Corsican. If the person was an American he'd profess to be French. And if then asked where he was born he'd tell him he was born in Corsica. French and Corsican. Being a patriot did not mean that he did not have universal beliefs, since Corsica itself was a rather tiny island and he was someone with much bigger ambitions than the island or his height might suggest. History books and Napoleon were mainly to blame for this.

But so was his father. He was a member of the Situationist International. He encouraged his son to pursue a degree in the environmental sciences at the University of Corte and to think of life as a series of spectacles. It was at the university that the Corsican led a group of conservationists in authoring a report on the state of the world's amphibians—but where was the value-added in that for Wayne, for whom nature was a disembodied view of Central Park South from a seventh-floor window table at Bergdorf? Wayne liked to go there without a reservation. This made the waiters run around in panic, whispering, "We have a window situation, we have a window situation . . ." which was one of his secret pleasures. Wayne liked these situations, for they said more about his social and economic status than the Situationists, whom he considered brain farts, for few of them had respect for money or the difficult work it took to make more and more of it. He met one such Situationist last year. He was a Breton who had studied philosophy at the Sorbonne.

"Why should I hire you?" asked Wayne.

"Because I'm committed to proving myself inside the citadel of capitalism," he said. "I'm a team player, I've stopped reading philosophy books and I'm prepared to work on weekends." But when Wayne asked him to calculate the enterprise value of a company, the brain fart just stared back.

"You need the fully diluted share count, it's in the income statement," Wayne finally said. "Then add the debt and back out the cash, basic stuff."

The philosophy major was about to cry.

The only company the Corsican ever worked for was Bustaci. He woke up early in the morning, picked up his axe, and went to work in a van with four other men. They made their way into the forest and at dusk they walked up to a dirt road, waiting for the van to pick them up again. Nature. He was in love with its prickly stems, its bramble and bush, the obstinate precision of its cycles, the coded tapestry of its patterns, the singular and undeviating silence of its hills, standing stubbornly in the way of human progress, but he had to do what he had to, and so every day he wielded his axe into nature. His father did the same before him, and so did his grandfather. They left Bonifacio and settled in the mountainous interior of the island to be near the factory, and so the Corsican had learned from a young age that beliefs do not always fall into universally accepted doctrines, and that sometimes one has no choice but to follow; that one has to set aside certain beliefs, or bend them, and do what one has to out of necessity in order to earn a living, yet when he took his axe to a tree he felt sickened by his condition. Wasn't that what had brought him here in the first place, this fervent desire to break away from the past in order to do things differently and for the better? This question was lodged in his head ever since he stepped into the MetLife Building. He wanted to get rid of it. He wished he was more like Simone Cordoba, like Dr. Wang, like that wizard of esoteric financial instruments, Pintu Banerjee. They were not encumbered by the dead weight of ideology. They simply did not have the time to be wistful or contemplative. They were not saddled by a nebulous desire to defend anything. Where was the value-added in that? They were there simply to make money. While he was stuck in these circuitous thoughts, another question brought him back to reality.

"Do you feel comfortable speaking English?" asked Wayne politely. "Because my Corsican is like shit."

"My English is fine."

"Good, good. My sales team says you're an investor. The intern says you're looking for a job. The answer to both is I can't help you out. The fund is now closed to new investors and we already have a full staff in place, so I'm not sure what you could do for us."

"I'd like to—"

"Before you go on, let me interrupt you for a second. Let me tell you about what we do here at Empiricus. It's actually quite simple. We use science to anticipate risk. We believe that there are immutable laws that govern the market: that the market is prone to crisis and that crisis pitilessly tears asunder the social ties that bind man to his fellow man, leaving no remaining other nexus between men than naked self-interest. I am thinking specifically of those types of men who make their living in the market. You may think that we are like them, but in reality we are quite different from them. We believe in betting against the market. We are convinced of its deterministic destruction. We don't like to take chances at Empiricus. God does not play dice.

"There are some things we like more than others. We like technology. We like progress. We don't like Enron, eToys, WorldCom. Fiber is for morons. We like bonds because so much of what determines their value is quantifiable. We are *quants* here at Empiricus.

"We believe that the scientific attitude is the critical attitude. We even had a resident physicist on staff. He believed in the Heisenberg principle. Ever heard of it? It's the theory that you cannot measure anything without affecting the measurement itself. In the end, we couldn't handle the uncertain outcome of such a hypothesis, so I fired him. It was a difficult decision for me. We favored his scientific approach but did not share his conclusions.

"Science is something we encourage here at Empiricus. We do not look for verifications but rather crucial tests. We are avid readers here. Everything we can get our hands on, except for literary fiction. It has no basis in mathematical reality. It is messy, imprecise, difficult to disprove. Are you with me? What else do we believe in . . ." It was more statement than question.

"We believe in the empirical content of the market. It gave us our name, Empiricus Kapital. We believe that there is truth in numbers. We believe in anticipating advances and declines. We believe that the economic motive pervades social life but that such a belief should not prevent us from making lots of money. We favor selling here. More than buying. Some accuse us of being biologically brooding, as if our parents carried Kafkaesque genes. But I grew up in a stable family: my father was a bridge-builder, my mom an accountant, and all around me there was a pervasive sense of order. They instilled in me a certain quest for precision, a love for exactness, which we try to emulate here at Empiricus. I had a happy, crisis-free childhood. Yet in the financial community they call me the Bleaker. I'm not *that* bleak, really. And I never bet blindly. We're not crazy Bears here who think the economy is going to be wiped off the map by Monday. That will take a little longer. One last thing you should know is that if for one reason or another all of the above does not bear out, we favor an activist approach when it comes to shaping market events. You may think that this is a cowardly disclaimer, but it is actually part of our hedging strategy. These general rules are the catechism of our trading. And you are hearing this from the high priest. Welcome to our temple, Empiricus Kapital. You are standing on hallowed ground here, scientifically speaking. But you may have already known this and perhaps you have come here for some other reason. If you've come here to ask for something, let me remind you about a rule we have here and I am sure you'll agree with me on the following fundamental postulate, namely, that there is no such thing as a free lunch in this here closed system called our universe. Are you with me?"

The Corsican thought about killing Wayne just to shut him up. "You don't have to sell me your product. I'm not an investor, but perhaps you can hire me and my friends. We are all out of a job."

"I'm sorry to say it, but this is kind of a nonstarter for me," Wayne responded. "Have you and your friends thought of going to a head-hunter?"

There was a diabolical asymmetry between the Corsican's cool countenance and the chaos of his thoughts.

"I used to work for Bustaci," he said.

Wayne smelled fear and opportunity in this revelation. He had been selling Bustaci shares for a while now. The information was out there in public filings for everyone to see. He was required to disclose his positions periodically in 13F filings. The number 13 was often followed by an F, a G or a D and in the coded language of Wall Street these documents were simply known as 13Fs, 13Gs or 13Ds. Seeing one on the Bloomberg unleashed unbridled passions. Stocks crashed or surged because of them. Fortunes were made or lost when it became evident that an important fund had cut back or increased its stake in a company. He didn't have anything personal against the number 13. It was just another prime number, no harm in that.

Wayne walked over to an antique globe at the corner of the conference room and slid his fingers along the sphere. "We have a nickname for this globe," he said, trying to buy time to assess the incremental bit of information the Corsican had shared with him. Was there an angle, an opportunity here?

"We call it Ploutos, the Greek word for wealth, and the countries you see here in North America are the envy of the world. We call them Plutonomies, countries characterized by capitalist-friendly governments and tax regimes, constant technological innovation, an embracing of globalization and immigration, financial innovation, the rule of law and patent protection, at least that is the general framework most of us live in, some sort of social contract most of us have bought into."*

The Corsican wondered whether Wayne would hire him and what it would be like to work for such an annoying personality.

Wayne's fingers crossed three emerging markets near the Caspian Sea: Azerbaijan, Armenia and Georgia. From the Caucasus they moved to the Balkans. He had trouble recognizing the nascent countries in this part of the world. Would their economies grow by more than 7 percent?

* From Bloomberg, "Citigroup's Kapur," by Michael Sesit, March 20, 2006. Kapur coined the term *plutonomy*.

"You must be upset that I am selling your company's shares," he finally said. "We used to be one of your largest holders, but then your management started doing stupid things and lumber prices started falling."

This was hardly privileged information. Empiricus had gone from net long to short in less than seven months and the first part of this trade was disclosed in the 13Fs. It was not his fault that lumber prices were plummeting or that Bustaci was teetering on the brink of financial ruin. The Corsican looked outside the double-glazed window. The sky was still cement gray.

"Tempu catt ìu," he said. "Bad weather."

3.

UNLIKE IN MANHATTAN, THE SKY in Marseille was crisp blue. The streets were empty, with the exception of trash and flying bits of paper. An unruly wind known as the mistral howled through the city. There were no signs of bourgeois orthodoxy in this working-class city. There was no stock exchange here. There was little indication of wealth or centralized power. Marseille was an impoverished port town, looking languidly across the Mediterranean. Immigrants dominated its center. Its buildings were faded and crumbling and there were few, if any, signs of gentrification. What the city lacked in bourgeois wealth it more than made up for in beautiful weather, but because of the wind Alix did not want to leave her apartment.

She walked to the kitchen and opened a plastic bag of candy. They came in psychedelic colors, resinlike miniatures representing the animal kingdom: tiny green bears, pink panthers, elliptical yellow eggs and orange camels. It was an unlikely coexistence, this rainbow alliance of creatures, yet they all converged inside shiny plastic bags unified under the company's marketing slogan: *"Haribo: C'est beau la vie, pour les grands et les petits."* She had been repeating it from the age of six, throwing a handful of candy into her mouth while she did. So her day had started off reasonably well. *Elle était contente. Elle voulait organiser une garden party, fêter ça avec un petit groupe de musique et un pique nique. La totale, quoi.* There was the sun. There was Haribo. The unemployment rate actually fell in March. Hail to the new prime minister. That was what the headlines in the papers said. But then she turned to page five of *Libération.* There was a review of a new book by an economics professor who had coined the term *anxiosphère* to describe the growing level of anxiety in French society. This *anxiosphère* was said to cast a stifling pall over not just France but the entire European Union. These were countries characterized by economic sclerosis, structural unemployment, social strife and lackluster labor markets. In short, absent the sun and the sea, they were difficult places to live. But this *anxiosphère* was not just confined to the core. It was said to be expanding to the outer provinces of the Continent. And it was not about to stop there. The word would eventually make its way into dictionaries, a sign that collective anxiety would enter the official lexicon of meaning.

Why were dictionaries getting so big anyway? There were new words sprouting every day to describe the same old world. Words like *gouvernance, anxiosphère* and *modalité.* People spoke of good governance, of multilevel governance, of proactive governance, but what did it all mean when she could not find a part-time job, when her rent subsidy shrank every year as if there were a mysterious correlation between the smaller checks she received and the thicker-than-ever dictionaries? Fifty years ago, the world according to an out-of-print edition of Larousse consisted of forty-seven thousand words. Today, it consisted of fifty thousand words. Even though some had fallen out of current usage, the rate of retention remained high, so that words accumulated on top of words, explaining, defining, amplifying, illuminating, elucidating, edifying and reinventing an ever-expanding reality obsessed by its own dilation. Yet to her the world was shrinking, as if certain meanings had fallen off the edge in the emptiness between space and science. Her teeth ripped into an orange camel. *C'est beau la vie.* Maybe life could be beautiful. Maybe Haribo was right all along.

Sometimes she walked to Hôtel Bellevue at ten in the evening for a free copy of the *Tribune.* That was where she first met the Corsican. He was always eager to see her. He showered her with compliments. "I want to make you my private revolution," he once said to her. And he did for a while. She was different from the women he knew, the ones from the island. They spent most of their time in the kitchen. They were prisoners of their own palaver. Their days were defined by domestic tasks. Their choices revolved around the olives they bought. They were earthbound, encumbered by the weight of tradition. He contemplated her posterior. It was lighter than lepton, the stuff of space. He wanted to knead his fingers into her.

The faded shutters of her apartment window swung wildly. With each burst of the mistral she imagined she was on a boat sailing toward Corsica. It was only when the winds retreated that she sat at her desk and turned her computer on. Her thoughts billowed and fragmented, rising above the island, this time moving away from the Mediterranean in the direction of the Atlantic. A few more keystrokes and she logged into her Hotmail account.

There was another email from Wayne.

These epistolary exchanges were half exciting, she thought, but when would they meet? She stood up and walked to the window. On Rue d'Aubagne an Algerian boy converged on a bouncing ball. What brought his parents to Marseille? Were they seduced by the sky, by the unruffled blue that encased the unrest below? She looked hopefully over the horizon. "Dear Wayne," she wrote, then hesitated. What should she write? Whatever you write, let him come to you, not you to him. It was always a good idea to start a letter with some general comments about the weather. "It's windy here but I'm going to be brave and go out and search for a tall building. Alix."

She then clicked on *send* and folded the sketch of a building she had drawn into her backpack. She put her coat on and left the apartment. It took her longer than usual to reach the hotel as she struggled to walk against the wind. On Rue d'Aubagne she entered a teahouse. The shop was dim and full of tired men stooped on little straw chairs. A ceiling fan ensured that there was a fair distribution of air. The men did not seem to notice that she was there. They were busy discussing the fate of Islam while sipping their tea. Marseille may have been a part of France, but here in this teahouse an army of defiant pastries had colonized the French. Maybe she was mad, *majnouna,* for coming here. By the time she reached the harbor the anchored boats facing Quai des Belges were struggling against the wind. It was more than four months that Alix and the Corsican had been meeting this way. And so what began as a casual encounter at Hôtel Bellevue grew into one of his most meaningful loves just as she was about to get rid of him.

Sometimes she bought him dinner at Le Pouce, after which they would walk back to the hotel and spend the night there before he took the ferry back to the island. When she saw him tonight he looked gray like a prehistoric slab of stone. On certain days he looked black like granite or assumed the calciferous color of the white cliffs at the southern tip of Corsica. He smelled like a forest. What did a forest smell like? Like tangles of trees and pink flowers, she would tell him. When she first met him he smelled of chestnuts, but lately he did not smell of anything.

They walked up the steps without saying a word and entered his room. They studied the sketch, after which he told her of the high forests in the isolated interior of the island. She had heard this story at least five times and could recite it by heart. She knew the names of all the books he had recommended she read. Interesting at first; she had read much worse. He had even given her a copy of the Situationist manifesto; she used it to smash an invading cockroach in her room, which was when theory lost the war against everyday living. Get a job, she told him, sweep away your island stories with a broom. Where is your ambition, where is your drive? "I'll show you my ambition, I'll show you my drive."

After they made love, which she went through with a certain tender resignation—she neither moaned nor yawned—they left the hotel and circled the harbor's periphery. She invited him for a drink at one of the tired bars of which there seemed to be many. The stores were empty and the only conversation they heard was the clatter of the shutters. She asked him what he would do with the sketch. The same as he did with all the others. He pinned them up on the walls of his home and studied them. He circled the ones he liked, the ones that would make the best spectacle.

A Theory of Deterministic Disaster

1.

IT WAS EIGHT IN THE EVENING and there was no one in the office except for Wayne. It was one of those days when God had abandoned the market, leaving traders exposed and exasperated. Stocks plunged, pushing the Dow to its sharpest drop in seven months in a sell-off sparked by International Business Machines. Benchmark indexes had their steepest declines since August and losses circled the globe amid renewed concern that Iran and Israel would go to war. Wayne was content, a knowing smile on his face.

When the market closed he began to plot his next target, leafing through the latest issue of *Architectural Digest,* a red pen in his hand. He placed the magazine down next to the Bloomberg and walked over to a full-length window, looking into the face of gravity. He was convinced that the Total Market Index, the broadest measure of U.S. shares, would soon fall off the edge of the world. All it needed was a nudge. He returned to his desk and placed the magazine under a stack of institutional reports. He leaned over his laptop and pressed a few keys. A chromatic scale appeared on a screen. In the lower left-hand corner was a graph with two plotted lines. One was restless; the other moved with predictable and measured undulations. Wayne considered the converging and diverging lines. It was difficult to concentrate. Ever since he had begun to email Alix, strange ideas occupied his mind. He wondered if human emotions could be charted in the same way that a government bond could.

He thought of Elizabeth Malkovitch, whom he'd met his sophomore year in college. During that cataclysmic year, Wayne fell in nonlinear love with Elizabeth, the type of love that is difficult to chart because it does not seem to be going anywhere. He discovered her inconstancy the same day of the ruble devaluation, which he now remembered more than Elizabeth. What crushed him at the time was the humiliating way in which he found out about her affair. He received an email attachment, a digital photo from the man who seduced her. The image was sent from the campus dormitory across from his. He was a medical student: a hairless Austrian with tentiginous triceps. His grandfather was a Nazi and he spoke English with a thick Teutonic accent. To make matters worse, the email subject field read: Elizabeth Malkovitch in Action. The attachment was titled takingitfrombehind.exe. He clicked on it. His beloved Elizabeth was on all fours. Her jaw was left hanging in what looked like a moan, the awfulness of it made worse by the low resolution. Wayne considered whether the attachment contained a malicious code, a disabling contagion of ones and zeros. He had learned one thing about caution from his protective father: that one could never be too cautious. Yet he had been eager to find out what the network nodes from half a world away had flushed down his inbox. There was a musical accompaniment that came with the attachment. It was, he later discovered, Wagner's *The Ring of the Nibelung.* But it was not all doom and gloom, or maybe it was. If it were not for Elizabeth Malkovitch, Wayne would never have developed his theory of deterministic disaster, which made him particularly attuned to the downside.

2.

HER NEIGHBORS RARELY COMPLAINED about the music Alix played, even in the canicular nights of July when their windows were left open to counter the heat. The music she listened to was an extension of the city: the sonorous signals of cell phones, the crusading call of the muezzin, the democratic drumbeat of pots and pans. The first Wednesday of the month was especially loud. Sepulchral sirens swirled at noon, sinking into the horizon, lost somewhere between sky and sea. Below her window on Rue d'Aubagne, teenagers carried boom boxes, milling about in oversized jeans. They spoke in *frablish,* a fusion of French, Arabic and English. Back in the insular warmth of her studio she put on a track from IAM. Unremitting beats bounced off the walls into unpredictable parabolas, then crashed into her ears:

Eille, Soleil, devient un violent poison
Pour ceux qui nous enferment derrière une cloison . . .

She turned her computer on, searching for an email from him: that slick stock operator from New York with the black silk shirt and suede boots, cocky and so full of himself. She thought he was trying too hard with the suede boots and laughed at him for it. He was the alpha male of email, but to say that this was the reason she first wrote to him would not be entirely true. She was given the task of asking him a few questions. Who was he exactly and how much was he worth? Who were the clients of Empiricus Kapital? Did he think that greed was good? If the emails failed, the Corsican asked her to talk to him once, no more than that.

Wayne had first come across her profile in his inbox. He was surprised to see an email from an Alix. Her name was equal in its distribution of vowels and consonants. It was a Roman name; that was obvious from the ending *ix*. The email contained a link that led to a portal. While exploring the site he came across an attachment; he clicked on it. It was a JPEG photo of a beautiful woman sticking out her tongue. She had a tiny birthmark on top of her upper lip. He zoomed into her pupil, then into her ear, then into her nose. As her features grew in size, the pixels faded into imprecise shapes.

Men and women usually met in bars, at cocktail parties or at the local diner. They met at the workplace, the university, through friends or friends of friends. He'd met one this morning in the pool inside the Time Warner Center. Thinking of her measured strokes, he was tempted to ask her out before leaving the gym. Her face was still a wet abstraction in his mind. There was hardly anyone at the pool that early in the morning. The world was sleeping, bunch of losers. Blood rushed to his brain's pleasure center. Electrical currents danced through a bundle of neurons about the size and shape of a peanut. Fortunately for the woman, Wayne's restless mind drifted to the stock market and his seat of reason, located in the brain's frontal cortex, reverted to a more modest set of expectations.*

Wayne minimized the JPEG photo on his screen and began to deconstruct the image. Her skin was diaphanous. A poignant network of veins appeared on her left temple. Her eyes were arctic blue but somehow never frozen. Her hair was long and

* This scientific reference is from Bloomberg, "Brain Scan of Traders Shows Link Between Lust for Sex and Money," by Adam Levy, February 1, 2006.

brown, the color of Corsican chestnuts. According to her profile, she came from a working-class family. Her father was a retired train conductor and her mother was an English language instructor and she grew up reading many novels.

He continued to read. Her stated goal in using the portal was to find an American friend to write to. He looked at the upper left-hand corner of the screen. A flashing box summarized her life. She was an architecture student. Below the box was a Sufi aphorism in black Arial font, her favorite condensed truth of the moment. "Love loves difficult things," it said. In addition to such nebulous fragments he also came across less lofty pieces of user information. He appreciated these the most. For example, she was last active on the site two days ago. She lived in the port city of Marseille. Her nationality was French. He did not hold this against her. A born-again positivist, he could not help but wonder how many of the pixels in the image had been doctored; if in reality she was not the bored housewife of an unfaithful professor. He was filled with doubt and for a second he thought of Elizabeth Malkovitch and his theory of deterministic disaster. Then an unusual piece of incremental information caught his attention. It was incremental because new information in finance is always referred to as such and this piece of incremental information was certainly value-added. Alix liked to walk on the rooftops of buildings. This precarious practice she had listed under hobbies; it had exposed her to vertical steel trusses, hydraulic jacks, hinged frames, weld blocks and lifting rods—in short, the structural dermatology of buildings, all of which she had enumerated in great detail. Wayne's poker face lost its delphic expression.

He kept her emails filed alphabetically by subject heading rather than by date, which denied the calendar its power in ordering things. When the market closed he stored her daily messages on CD to give him a better margin of safety. In one email titled Planet Mars, she wrote:

> Life seems to be lived on the edge at the moment, everywhere. We hold our breath, wait, worry, fear that which is to come and live carefully. Except for me. I was stuck the other day at Metro Belsunçe in a great immovable mass. I pushed myself out into the marketplace. I looked for the tallest structure around me. I climbed up the hill in the direction of Cours Julien. I rang all of the apartments in a pastel-colored residential building. Someone finally let me in. I walked five flights up a narrow spiral staircase and accessed the roof. I went across a cantilevered steel bridge spanning the gap between two buildings. Then I looked across to the views of the city framed by housing projects, then down to the courtyard. There were people lunching at Le Jardin d'Acôté. Others were dealing drugs, begging for money. I sprawled on the red tiled bricks baking under the sun. Later on, before dinner, I went to my

> yoga class and for the first time I was able to do the crow pose correctly. The world around me is falling apart but I feel soooooo good, like something new is about to begin, but enough about me. I wonder how you are, how goes the trading?
>
> Kisses, Alix . . .

In one of his more sentimental exchanges he responded:

> The fund is performing well. We continue to stick to our proven game plan of bottom-up fundamental research to help predict the sustainability of future cash flows. As I write this, my colleagues are looking at the financials of a Corsican company to understand the variability of its returns and the use of its capital. You may have heard of them, Bustaci. They're a multinational based in Corsica, birthplace of Napoleon, with plans of world conquest that make his pale in comparison. They make corrugated cardboard boxes, as if our lives would be marginally incomplete without them. Our analysis has concluded that industry trends are eroding their position, and so we're betting that this fad, this pathetic paper company, will go down the way of the pet rock, i.e., bankrupt. In our experience (a cumulative twenty-two years of graduate study, five languages and more than three billion in assets under

management), we have found that a number of stocks in the market trade within +/-25 percent of their fair value, or of fair market value. We only like to invest when we find stocks that are outside the 25 percent value range. Bustaci is one. It trades in the +37 percent range, ripe for a fall. As Newton so aptly put it, "What goes up must come down." I am paraphrasing, of course. For a more technical explanation you may want to read up on the second law of thermodynamics, which states that the quality of energy is degraded irreversibly. This is the principle of the erosion of energy, which can also be applied to the stock market, another closed system just like the totality of the universe.

Anyway, I'm probably boring you with all this stuff.

Lousy weather here today. The barometer is a bitch, the AC is down, and they forgot the tomato in my avocado sandwich.

Asta la vista, baby.
And kisses to you too,

Wayne$

3.

AFTER THE CLOSE, Jatin Kumar, yet another Indian analyst from Bear Stearns, raised his price target on Bustaci. Old numbers were excavated and thrown out. New ones were considered. Perhaps predictability was really short-term, just like the weather. Wayne dragged his mouse to the upper right-hand corner of his screen and double-clicked on a file called Alix. She had sent a total of twenty-one emails during the fiscal year. He thought about charting them. Many of them contained detailed descriptions of the buildings she visited. He took meticulous notes of the structures, setting them aside for further research.

In one of her emails she wrote:

Dear Wayne,

When was the last time you walked on the rooftop of the Centre Pompidou? When was the last time you went to the beach? When was the last time you slept next to a Frenchwoman instead of counting your money? Eat an urchin. Look down. Fall in love. Live a little.

Je t'embrasse,

Alix

Wayne smiled. The last time he went to the beach was at the Hamptons, where even the pigeons were a monochrome white. He drove up in a polychrome gray SUV like many of the other Wall Street professionals who spent their weekends tooling their boats to forget their benchmarks. Before he drove to the beach that day he went for an early swim to make sure that the resilience of his flesh matched that of his will. It was a pleasant weekend away from Wall Street, away from the digital rivers of red and green. And on his way back to the city he stopped at a café on Mott where two patrons talked about Enron while tucking into their oven-baked sunny sides. Back then, before the market tanked, the city was full of optimists. Wayne was quite contemptuous of them because they made their money the easy way during the Long Boom. It was the decade when people worked the Web, fed the hype and exploited the buzz. It was the era of precision accountability.

Absolute morons, Wayne thought. They should all be zapped.

He just wanted to get away, in space and time. He looked at his watch. The sun was setting in Marseille. Alix stood on the roof of a neoclassical building on Rue de la République. At one end of the titanic street was the Old Port. At the other was Place Sadi-Carnot. The downward-sloping, sinking avenue was her favorite in the city. She considered the imperial buildings along the length of the street, reflecting on the French predilection for axis. Wayne too organized his thoughts with Haussmann-like rigor.

In one of his emails he wrote:

I don't have time to go to the beach or walk on the rooftop of the Pompidou Center. I spend my weekends toying with computational certainty. The other day I was experimenting with a Monte Carlo simulations program in order to quantify our chance meeting under different political regimes. And guess what? You may think of our meeting as fateful, but I did everything I possibly could to minimize the fate factor. I am sorry for this. I am just puzzled by one thing. You claim to be French, but your written English is so good. Are you a statistical aberration, a black swan type of event? The few French people I know are very bad with foreign languages.

To which Alix responded by raising the possibility of a certain ex-lover, who happened to be Corsican, and by doing so, lifted her position on the demand curve:

Mon Wayne,

It is good to hear from you, but can you lay off the probability stuff a little? I'm not sure I should mention this to you, but I want to be completely open about everything, not that you have solicited any special kind of information from me. I just came back from seeing my sort of ex-lover. I say sort of because he doesn't quite know that it is over. No, I didn't meet him while studying architecture at the university. What happened was that we had a messy argument and now he's depressed. I left him in his hotel room, drinking his beer and watching the India-Pakistan cricket match. *Mon dieu,* I hope that it's not going to be the beginning of another Bollywood serial. I couldn't take it. I've had enough of him. When we make love I can't help but smell the *figatelli* in his sticky beard, the insistent smell of that brazen sausage wafting through the sordid restaurants I invite him to because he's out of a job and broke. At least I no longer smell him. I'm sorry to bother you with this. I just want you to know everything about me. Well, not everything, but I feel it's easy to share things with you, maybe because I don't know you. And I want to tell you that I feel lucky to have met you. I think we would have met anyway. Have you heard of a thing called fate?

As for my English, I agree that it is quite good. For that I have my mother to thank—she's an honorable Englishwoman—and also my dear English professor at the Institute and many tedious years of doctoral study at the École d'Architecture, where I'm now working on a new architectural response to the problem of collective housing. This is what takes me on my expeditions to the rooftops of buildings. I'm not sure if this disqualifies me from being a black swan, but I do like to think of myself as a rare bird, an ominous, ravenous swan that will swoop down over New York City soon. So make sure that you make contingency plans. I'm crisis incarnate in all of its shapes and forms.

Prends soin de toi et ecris-moi de longs mots, de longs mots d'amour.

Kisses,

Alix

I'm sorry about your friend [he wrote]. I am not sure what to tell you, except that you probably should avoid the topic of the India-Pakistan cricket match when you talk to him. It's a sour point for Pakistan this week. The entire country is depressed and many disillusioned fans, I understand, have set themselves on fire. I sort of feel a little sorry for them myself. I mean, they lost by nine wickets, and for the deciding third test next week they will be without their all-rounder, the highly respected Abdul Razzaq, who is suffering from a groin problem. I expect their productivity rate to be down for the month and therefore have been betting against their currency.

Is your ex Pakistani?

If you really feel like talking I can offer you my cell, though you should know that I'm not a big fan of phones, cell phones in particular, with their tendency of multiplying and facilitating *other* discourses, which make human connection thoughtless and easy. Why don't you just send a text message to my BlackBerry?

She was not sure what a BlackBerry was:

Mais non, my sort-of-ex is not at all Pakistani, I don't want to talk about it. It's bad luck to talk about exes. I know it may seem very un-French of me to be unambiguous, but I just want you to know that I'm not seeing him or anyone else at the moment. I am actually feeling a bit down today, and not just because of him. There was a devastating accident at the football stadium yesterday. I saw it from the rooftop of the Corbusier Building, which I happened to be on at the time. I go there often in the summer months right before the guard locks up the roof and I spend the entire night there, counting the stars. I like to look north when I am on top of this particular building, into the wilderness of the city, where colossal housing projects threaten to overtake the surrounding mountains. I stare at the flickering lights of the distant apartment blocks through twisted branches and shivering leaves. This time there was no wind and it was not quite dark. I heard a loud cracking noise followed by a whooshing sound. When the noise stopped, the arena threw up a cloud of debris in the air, tossing out human bodies right and left. I knew then that there was something wrong with the intermediate diagonals. I am not suggesting that this was an engineering problem. I have looked at the plans of the stadium. They are structurally sound. I fear a bomb may have knocked off the vertical posts above the top nodes of the space frame. The authorities are still investigating the cause, but it is pretty clear to me what happened. This was no accident. You should have seen the manic crowd bursting out of the gates. People ran down Boulevard Michelet, a diabolical swarm of delirious flesh. I should go now, the siren is sounding. They want everyone downstairs . . .

Je te tiens au
courant.

AL

Stay calm [he wrote]. Here is my cell: 9175555378. Call me if you need anything, and don't think I'm getting overly sentimental, but I understand your pain. Bad day in the market today. The S&P 500 soared more than two percentage points. Corning Inc., the world's largest maker of glass used in flat-panel televisions, reported earnings that surpassed forecasts. We are screwed today. The world looks a little safer. The heater is down again and this time the deli forgot the avocado in my avocado sandwich. It's just not my day.

Asta lavista for now.

Das Kapital $$

Does he actually think that he is more stressed than me? she thought, and so she drafted a litany of complaints to see whether he would offer help or even cared.

Dear Das,

I am trying to stay calm. It's not easy. The Bikram yoga classes I take do me no good. I walk out of class, not a single knot in me, and after an hour my body consents to reality's domination. I tense up again. Plus I am having money problems at the moment, the life of a struggling student. Fortunately, my friend, the one I told you about, repaid his debts and gave me an extra 1,000 euros. I'm not sure where his money is coming from, but it certainly is not going to win back my love or loyalty. I'll call you soon. In the meantime tell me something about yourself, something personal. Do you like to read French fiction, because if you do I can recommend some very good books perhaps? I don't know anything about you.

The flurry of emails continued and with each passing day the memory of the granite island faded in her mind. A new island had begun already to vitiate the memory of the old one. It was not particularly painful to forget the Corsican. He was a bit of a brute, a wild man of the maquis. The pundits of good taste would say nothing but sloppiness and poverty. In economic terms the Corsican favored the many over the few, the cult of quantity-over-scarcity value. He showered her with many compliments, repaid his many debts and offered her many gifts, including one diamond ring she threw away in the back of her drawer somewhere.

Couldn't they just be friends?

"I've found a job," he told her. "Let me take you out to dinner."

"No, thanks," she said. "Save your money, wherever it's coming from."

Their fateful meetings at Hôtel Bellevue would soon become coincidental and the coincidental would fade into the routine and the routine would morph into a casual moment or two, moments whose coordinates would be difficult to plot. Wasn't that what happened over time? Yet to him she was as constant as the sun.

> *How the earth is nubile and rich in blood and how it contains, big in sap and rays of light, the vast swarming of all embryos. The Sun the hearth of tenderness and life.*

It was not every day that a Corsican recited Arthur Rimbaud to a woman from Marseille. The first time he did was during a walk along the coast that took them to a modernist monument built in Rimbaud's honor. It stood strangely on a mound of grass, facing the sun and the sea, a reminder of his peripatetic life as poet and trader until he died a sick man in the port city. She appreciated the fatalism and poetry of the story, but were there not many suns in a universe, not just the one mentioned in this particular poem? And was it so difficult to imagine a universe without this particular Corsican, whose unbending beliefs and maudlin love letters written in pen seemed so much more impractical and spindly than the energizing burst of electronic mail? All that she could think about was her inbox and another message from Wayne. In one of his emails he confessed to having read fiction.

> I'm terribly busy [he wrote]. The market is about to close and I have to meet a client. I am out the door at two to four. Okay then, something personal about me: I hate it when they forget the tomato in my avocado sandwich. I hate it when the market goes up. And I have never shared this with anyone, but yes, I once tried to read the French writer Georges Perec. I mean, who would ever consider writing a book without using the letter E?
>
> Diabolical, mathematical, scientific. He's a brainiac, Perec, but I still couldn't finish the book. Otherwise, I've skimmed through Kafka and Kundera, but neither really helps you become a better trader. There is absolutely no upside in literature.
>
> It's twenty past four, I'm out the door.

I'm so excited that we have found something in common. [Her heart fluttered like an equatorial butterfly.] I agree that E is one of the most overused letters in the romance languages. My favorite letter remains the deeply misunderstood X. To me, it is more than two slanted I's crossing each other. X lacks the uptight posture of the letter I. It is blissfully free of its singular determinism. Yet it also avoids the sloppiness of the S, its unreliable meanderings and curves. I see X as two tired lovers, really, fallible and incomplete, so that they each hold on to the other for sustenance and support. And this one letter X is full of so much meaning, multiple meanings that are shrouded in mystery. It is the Roman numeral 10. It's a film rating to designate pornographic content. In mathematics, it is an unknown quantity, also a sign for multiplication. It is a chromosome in my body and the last letter of my name. I am deeply attached to it.

X of Provence.

He preferred numbers to letters, not for their shapes but because they represented quantity and because, unlike words, he trusted the constancy of a fraction more than the disloyalty of the alphabet. "Sure thing," he wrote three days later, "I'll write longer."

"Something terrible has happened in Marseille," she wrote.

"Outside my window the black clouds are moving in abundance; thunderous oblivion, a continual breaking of the sky."

That should get his attention.

"Don't worry," he wrote, "bad weather, probably. Take a look at Italy. A powerful bomb exploded in the Basilica di San Marco, sending the Treasury yield curve into inversion. Banerjee, our resident analyst, is trying to establish correlation.

"Gotta go. Market's like a yo-yo."

Was this guy for real? She clipped her toenails before returning to her laptop.

"I have no idea what you are talking about," she gave up. "I'm trying to visualize an inverted yield curve. The only thing I come up with is an advanced yoga posture. Are you making or losing money because of this inversion?"

"I am making money, absolutely. The market just buckled and everything is going down. Some brain fart on CNBC is saying that it's because corporate earnings were weak. Hell-o. I mean, WHERE HAVE YOU BEEN? Sony Ericsson just reported that their second-quarter profits dropped 61 percent as the price of handsets fell. Handset schmandset. It's a free fall. Live cattle futures are dead. There is no future."

"Whatever you say (yawn), honey . . . I am going to ride my bike to the farmers' market at Cours Julien. The Corsican cheese is to die for. Will write longer. In the meantime, try to clean up your mouth a little. I can do without the vulgarity."

He wrote to her again after the market close:

"Sorry for being so excited. Everyone has left the office and

I feel calmer. Below my window I can see tiny Yellow Cabs streaming down Park Avenue. They are fading into the night. So here is something else about me. I think you asked how I became interested in the structural aspects of buildings. It started with the Basilica. I first visited the Basilica and the campanile next to it as a university student. The bell tower was said to be the highest structure in Venice. Everything has come down now. We first found out about the bombing from the numbers. That's how we always find out about things. It's always the numbers. They come crashing down in their quiet, septic way so that we come out with our hands clean. I knew something terrible had happened when I looked at the tape. That was the first indication. That's always the first indication. I did not need to listen to the news. I don't believe what the talking heads say, that it was because of earnings, that it was because of the handhelds. It was not because of the earnings. It was not because of the handhelds. It was because of the Basilica. I did not have to turn on the radio. I knew that this would happen. I was prepared for it. I am trying to remain calm now, opportunistic. I still remember the glittering façade of the church, the exotic Byzantine architecture, the gold mosaics covering the ceilings and walls, the marble floors, the five vaulted domes, which formed the roof in the shape of a Greek cross. All of it gone now, and in place of the dome is a gaping hole."

"Well, Wayne, we studied the Basilica last semester," she wrote. "They started work on it in the ninth century. It was built with an Eastern and Byzantine influence. Some three hundred years later they completed the magnificent domes. It took one explosion to wipe away all of that. It's disgusting."

"You don't know what disgusting is," he wrote in an IM. "Let's not talk about this anymore. Tell me, when are we going to meet?"

City of Dreams

1.

TWO WEEKS LATER THEY MET at Balthazar. It was packed with smart, sybaritic New Yorkers. Wayne emerged from the crowd in a white summer suit, 190-gauge tropical wool, which he had bought at Barneys. His shirt was light to the point of transparency, yet just durable enough to be stitched without tearing. His face was determined, as if it had a duty toward ambition or some other attainable cause. He had no noticeable identifying marks on his face, no scars or wrinkles.

"I thought you would like it here," he said. "It's a good introduction to Gotham." She was excited when he ordered snails. Her cultural receptors had been conditioned to champion the terrestrial gastropods from an early age. They may seem sluggish and slimy, she thought, but there is something sexy about snails.

When she first saw him he was everything that she had imagined. He looked a little postcoital, though he'd just come from work. His hair was messy; his eyes were a little tired, red and disinterested. It seemed as though he was getting a lot of sex; whether he was or not was secondary. He certainly didn't look like he was begging for it. He challenged the world with his testosterone (and aftershave). Whatever it was, the smell sent her olfactory transmitters on a Proustian journey into the past, into her aunt's country house in the Lubéron, where she went every June to pick strawberries and lie supine under the sun. It was a musty, penetrating smell that evoked the wild passions of the SAS novels that she had read. They resided somewhere between the forbidden and the forgotten until the scent of his fragrance projected the past into the palpating present, so that she wanted to make love to him right there and then in front of everyone.

"What's that you have on?" she asked.

"Chanel, for men. New and Improved," he said. "I knew you'd like it."

Such confidence, she thought. A true alpha male emeritus. He offered unmatched versatility with restrained sensitivity, *a winning combination.* When she first set eyes on him it was apparent that he was a fervent proponent of cardiovascular training, that he could do 150 crunches a day, legs on an armchair. He ran regularly, jumped rope and rode a bike. She was certain that he had StairMaster thighs, cloaked under his trousers.

So far, so good.

Then he smiled and it was the last piece of evidence she needed: the perfect man with perfect teeth with durable dentin and enamel. During dessert he would confide that he never had orthodontic braces. She had dated someone with gingivitis and found it terribly annoying. It was a sensitive question to ask, but she wondered if he had all thirty-two of his teeth intact. Of course he had all thirty-two of his teeth intact, white as a polar bear. The angulation of his teeth was perfect. In a moment of openness he shared with her the toothpaste he used. It was Marvis, imported from Italy: *alito fresco per tutto,* which he recited in front of the bathroom mirror, laughing on the rest of humanity. He had also mastered the art of shaving. He used a stainless steel razor and a pure badger brush with a faux ivory handle.

Her heart skipped a beat.

He was Wonderful, Ineluctable. She bumped her knee against his leg. His pupils dilated. She looked at him. He had a symmetrical face, a jutting chin firmer than Gibraltar, yet his skin was tender-soft like an innocent yearling.

He inhaled deeply. There was pheromone in the air, pheromone unbound, flying vicariously. They looked at each other in a daze. He wished he had a device similar to a konimeter, an instrument with wondrous wiring and friendly ergonomics to collect samples of dust in the air, except that this new device would capture the airborne pheromone, scientific, empirical proof that there was something happening between them. He smiled; his chin was still jutting, firmer than Gibraltar. She found his smile winning. She wanted him. But first she hoped he would put his hand on her knee. He cupped his hand around her knee, snugly, as if he had read her mind. He was truly exceptional, the embodiment of the universe. But could he cook?

"Do you always eat in expensive restaurants?" she asked, holding her breath.

"It depends." He was being misty, mysterious. "I tend to think that food is overrated, but yeah, I suppose I can cook a little. The other day I did this salad: dandelion with other pleasantly bitter greens. Then I added bits of Canadian bacon, shavings of Gruyère cheese, chopped egg . . ."

It was when he said "egg" that he reached over the table and held her hand. This move was clearly strategic. He had read somewhere that the sense of touch opened the floodgates to oxytocin and that higher levels of oxytocin resulted in greater sexual receptivity in the nipples and penis. There was speculation in scientific journals that oxytocin was also responsible for increasing sperm count. He was eager to test this theory.

She did not frown upon his positivism. Time was the real test of love, she thought, not sperm count. But she did not make an issue of it. She pressed his hand. She felt a frisson in her fragile body: a trembling that penetrated the aggregate of her tissues. Would he try to kiss her before the end of the night? She found herself shrouded in a pall of persistent happiness. It must be the neurotransmitters agitating in her body, Wayne thought, the endorphins swimming excitedly inside of her. In time he would come to recognize the singular, transcendent power of love, she thought, which was beyond them, in spite of them, like an enchanting Sufi moment that had suffused them with all that was in the universe, drawing upon them the observing eyes of this world.

2.

HE SWALLOWED MORE SNAILS and surveyed the irrationally exuberant crowd. Nowhere else could one find such a heady mix of downtown spectaculars feasting on caviar redolent of the Caspian Sea.

"It's all happening right now and it could only happen here," he said.

She smiled and succumbed to the caviar, rubbing the black eggs against her gums. When dinner arrived, they both went through it with procedural alacrity. She did not finish her seared duck breast. He looked bored with his collard greens. It was time to pay the bill. She expected him to pay with cash. He charged it on plastic.

"There was a time when Yap islanders kept huge stones in front of their homes," he said. "The size of the stone indicated how rich you were. We've used beads, silver and gold since then, and now we use paper and call it money. But money can take up so much room, which is why I prefer to use plastic."

What an intelligent, historical man. When it was time to leave, he held her jacket for her in a courtly manner. And when he finally held the restaurant door, she felt as though he had metamorphosed into a gentleman scholar that recalled an earlier era. He seemed transported from the pages of a novel by Stendhal.

Inside the cab their lips met for the first time. It was not a Hollywood kiss; it was a tectonic collision prompted by the driver slamming the brakes. And then Wayne saw something beyond him, a luminous atom suspended between their lips. In a wink, the restless, bouncing infinitesimal multiplied into a billion subatomic particles, a quantum kaleidoscope that filled the dark empty space between them.

"Ouff," she said, *"mon Dieu!"*

He stared outside the backseat window of the cab. His eyes caught a Starbucks ad on a billboard looming over the highway: "Coffee. Community. Camaraderie. Connection."

She unbuttoned his pants and nestled her head between his thighs. "I want you to express yourself," she said. He looked outside the window into the neon-lit night. The driver accelerated past another billboard, determined to escape its reproachful gaze. Wayne still managed to read the text: "We Are Not

Evolution's Final Product, Just Light-Years Ahead of the Rest. Matrix CD-Writer: The Drive to Be Your Best." By the time they passed the glorious McDonald's arches she was in a half-tortoise pose taking in a deep breath. His fingers crawled like a caterpillar over the back of her head. He caressed her hair, longer than the West Side Highway. Her head moved back and forth in a rhythmical, dialectical dance. "Express yourself," she said.

He was about to, but before he could, she woke up to the sun; bright spots dappled on her face. She rubbed her eyes and rolled out of bed. It was seven in the morning and the sun emerged over the white, gnarled hills in the distance. Marseille was still asleep, submerged in its own dream. The only noise came from a *mobylette,* hurtling into the unknown. Then a Berber boy in drooping jeans appeared in the middle of the street, a ghetto blaster planted on his shoulder.

Better get some work done before he played Sister Souljah.

But first she walked over to the kitchen to prepare some tea: a blend of smoky souchong and gunpowder-grade oolong. As the water simmered, she powered her laptop and dragged her cursor onto a JPEG on the desktop. It contained technical drawings of several bridges designed by Santiago Calatrava. Wayne had asked her to send him some of the sketches and she eagerly compiled a list. Among them was the breathtaking Bach de Roda built for the Olympic Games in Barcelona; the

Alamillo, which was commissioned for the World's Fair in Seville; and the Campo Volantin in Bilbao. She worked until noon, when she heard a throbbing noise outside her window. She stuck her head out and screamed at the boys below. They were listening to NTM* from a big black boom box.

"Will you turn down the volume?" she shouted.

"Ferme ta gueule, salope," one of them promptly answered, *"si non je vais te fumer."*†

Perhaps she should have anguished more over the possibility of finding a common language. But then what would they talk about? And what would she talk about with the Corsican? They shared a language but no longer a converging desire. She did not want to meet him tonight. Would he invite her out for a bite? Would he ask her up to his room? Would they talk about environmental doom?

On her way to the hotel, Alix stopped by the teahouse on Rue d'Aubagne. The patrons played backgammon under a resigned lightbulb. They dunked their worries in their tea, then pulled them out for everyone to see. When she ordered a pastry, they offered her a plate of three.

"Vous allez me faire grossir," she said. You're going to make me fat.

* Nique Ta Mère

† "Shut your trap, bitch, or I'll smoke you out."

"Koul, koul," the owner said in Arabic. Eat, eat. *"Comme t'es chewat."*

The ceiling fan worked at double speed while time stood still. At Hôtel Bellevue, the Corsican stood in front of the door facing the port, with a monastic expression on his face. Then he saw her in the distance and waved. His face became animated and his eyes grew big. He now stood facing her, waiting for her parsimonious kiss. But when he leaned forward she turned away so that she now faced the Notre Dame cathedral. An anchored boat in the harbor made a peculiar noise, or perhaps it was the fisherman inside carrying a bucket of fish. Though the Corsican could not see its contents, just as he could not see into Alix's mind, he imagined that it was full of blood.

"What's wrong?" she asked.

"Nothing, I'm just a little nervous," he said. "Let's go up to my room and take a look at your sketch."

"I forgot to bring it," she said. "I'll make sure to bring it next time, and I'd like to go up, but I can't tonight. I have a school project I'm working on."

"Fine," the Corsican said, "but I'd like to know if you're seeing someone."

"Yeah, sure," she said, "I'm seeing myself and spending far too much time at home working on this project and making love to mysterious foreign men, mostly in my dreams. I just want to be alone."

"Everyone is alone," the Corsican said.

3.

WAYNE ANXIOUSLY READ her notes about the bridges. She had also sent him a JPEG file of the structures. On first glance they looked simple, but there was a lot of complexity there. He threw away a printout of the first photo. It was a drawing of the Bach de Roda built in a poor neighborhood of Barcelona. There was not much urban activity around the bridge, which was located in a kind of *bidonville.*

He turned his attention to the Bloomberg. A flood of light covered his screens. The sun came in from all sides through the glass windows. He could hardly see. He felt heavy thinking about the heat. He dropped a tablet of Supradyne in a glass of water to boost his level of energy. He typed MSFT, the symbol for Microsoft, into the Bloomberg, followed by the <equity> key. The Supradyne fizzled in the water. He took a sip of the urine-colored liquid and felt like throwing up. The reflection of an integer evanesced in his iris, then another whole number took its place. He put his aviator glasses on to protect his eyes from the unrelenting sun. Microsoft was up more than a dollar. It was not easy being a short-seller. If most investors suffered from a naive optimism, Wayne had always thought of himself as a pragmatic realist. He despised most of the investment community: the sell-side, the buy-side, the day traders, the slick stock promoters who spoke with the illusion of knowledge.

Their thought process was immutable, immutably flawed. They believed that stock prices would move ever higher. They were spuriously irrational, driven by imitation and moronic behavior. Wayne could not share their buoyant optimism. One thing that world history teaches us is that disaster will befall one who hangs around long enough. In this inevitability Marx was right. If he could only go back in a time machine to trade on the October Revolution, the assassination of JFK, the Yom Kippur War. He had the cunning of a great political thinker. He preferred to make money from disaster.

Then the United States dropped bunker bombs on Syria and after so much waiting Wayne felt vindicated. Swap spreads fluctuated wildly. Bond prices surged as if the gods of science had issued a fatwa on the stock market. There simply weren't any buyers. He had predicted it all with mathematical certainty. The Dow shed 315 points, the tech-laden Nasdaq closed down 91 points. In an act of desperation, a trader jumped off the roof of the MetLife Building. Wayne waited patiently for the next global failure, a so-called ten-sigma event: a statistical freak occurring one in every ten to the twenty-fourth power times. The ten-sigma was imminent, if not today then tomorrow, if not tomorrow then in a year, if not in a year then in a century or an even later point in time. It did not matter when. Sooner or later the mother of all disasters would strike, and if it did not happen during his life, then that was okay. There would be many little disasters in between that he would witness. Yet even this reassuring thought did not make him feel better. The cumulative weight of the numbers he had seen depressed him: a perpetual repository of fractions, losses and gains, of quiet trading days and standardized logarithmic returns. It was stupid to ascribe meaning to this cemetery of numbers. It was stupid to talk to a computer screen. It was stupid to not fall in love. He shut his computer off. He slipped into his yellow Patagonia and stepped into the elevator. In the lobby, Mike Bartalos, the Hungarian night guard, with two American flags pinned to his chest, smiled, a Protestant-ethic smile he had ably integrated into his greeting. Though he had emigrated from a country that was overwhelmingly Catholic, corporate America had remade him into its own.

"You're working late today," he said in a supportive voice.

"Not as late as you," Wayne shot back. "I'll see you early in the morning."

"Sure thing, chief, see you in the morning."

Outside the building he was confronted by a giant bull, an orange bull that had no basis in reason or reality. It was as though the Surrealists had taken over the city. There were fiberglass sculptures of bulls all over Manhattan. Bulls in orange-red, pastel pink and vermilion. Another esoteric art project sponsored by the city in the name of the public good. Like a resigned matador, he walked around the bull and stepped into the street. A fleet of Yellow Cabs passed by, fading into the night. He waited for nearly five minutes before one pulled over. From the backseat of the cab he threw a bored look at the driver's nameplate. Boris Tereschenko. Great. Another Ukrainian, he thought, trying to scrape by in the Big Rotten Apple. Wayne hoped that he would keep his mouth shut. The ones who talked the most were always angling for a tip. Either that or they were eager to point out how much smarter they were than their backseat client; that driving a cab was not *really* their true calling, that it was beneath them, that they had dropped out of a PhD program in computer engineering, having realized that there was more to life than longitudinal redundancy checks. Whatever. Just get me to where I want to be. Tereschenko looked in the rearview mirror.

"Downtown," Wayne said. "The strip club in the Meatpacking District."

Tereschenko pressed on the accelerator.

"Their lease expired last month," he said. "They've moved to the West Side Highway."

Wayne was not a regular at the club. He liked this one because the bathrooms did not smell of semen and Mr. Clean. He derived less pleasure with each visit. He recalled one of his earlier lessons in economics, the theory of declining marginal utility. The professor had used the example of a chocolate bar to make his point. Although for every extra Mars bar someone eats they derive extra pleasure, the more Mars bars that are eaten, the less the pleasure gained from each incremental one. Is paying money to stare at a naked body more or less the same? There is always the first, but then comes the second, the third and so on, until the fetishized objects of our desires devolve into a tired repetition of themselves.

Wayne felt bored as the cab reached its destination. He stepped into the cool night wind; it hovered over the Hudson, brushing against his Windbreaker. At the entrance he paid ten dollars in exchange for a gold coin. Inside the club a tall nude girl was dancing onstage, touching her pussy as if it were disembodied. A silver ring hung from her right nipple, a dog collar around her neck. The music was old school, East Coast. It was Slick Rick blaring from Samsung speakers: *Cover your mouth because you almost choke, you see the mailman's dick way up your wife's throat . . .*

Wayne reached into his pocket for a twenty-dollar bill. Just then his cell vibrated. "*Salut mon lapin,* where are you, sweetie?" It was X of Provence. He got up and left, a smile on his face. His twenty dollars were irretrievable, a sunken cost, but he felt strangely reassured. He hoped there was only one Alix and that she did not have a double. He hoped that one day he would have the opportunity to meet her, to count the constellation of freckles on her back. He had this unlikely urge to do this over and over again, perhaps a million times over, in defiance of the theory of diminishing marginal utility. "I arrive a week from today," she said. "Are you ready to receive me?" To which Wayne responded, "What are you doing up so early? Has the mayor declared another state of emergency? And yes, I am ready to receive you."

Made in New York

1.

THEY FIRST MET AT BALTHAZAR—and this time it was not a dream. He could have made a better choice. Another French brasserie in New York, she thought, trying hard to be another French brasserie in New York. She ordered a glass of pastis, the ersatz absinthe she liked so much because of its cloudy, ambiguous color. Wayne emerged from the crowd in a crisp pin-striped shirt. His top collar button was open. His face resembled a Greek philosopher's, at times taciturn, at other times animate, always deliberate and configured to trigger a predetermined response.

"Would you like some *moules frites*?" he asked.

"I like the way you pronounce *moules,*" she said. "You seem so cosmopolitan."

Wayne, however, was not that well traveled, and he was certainly not a man of the cosmos. The world he knew was the world of the atlas. He took the *Universalis* with him every time he went to the bathroom. The atlas looked heavily used. There were index cards sticking out from its edges with notes and Greek letters denoting Euclidian equations. There were arrows connecting one continent to another. There were roman numerals enumerating the dimensions of bridges he had drawn on maps. He memorized the names of rivers just as he had the batting averages of certain baseball players. Sitting on the toilet, one of his favorite tasks was to identify high-density cities and measure their distance to regional conflicts. He would then superimpose all of this data on a Treasury yield curve. He would do the same for strategic cities outside the *alliance,* starting from the periphery and tracing his way back to the *metropole.* From Kabul to New York, always drifting from the edges to the core in precise concentric circles. Apart from these mental travels he had only been to Italy as a wide-eyed exchange student. Yet his knowledge of urban planning was global. He collected architectural drawings of factories, the headquarters of multinationals, totemic power towers and industrial parks.

When she first saw him she wondered if there was something wrong with him. His hair was messy. His eyes were agitated. They moved back and forth like a broken pendulum. Soon after, the waiter brought the mussels and the smell of Brent Crude oil filled the air. The last time she had mussels it was at a restaurant near the Étang de Berre, a pond of dubious hygienic quality, with a high concentration of oil refineries in its proximity. They might have looked seductive, she thought, but there was something subaltern and suspicious about them.

He unfolded the napkin on the table, placed it neatly on his lap and picked a mussel with measured grace. Like an algorithm, every detail about him made sense. She was determined to find a personal failing to confirm his humanity. Wayne turned his attention to the two Wall Street bankers at the table next to theirs. An archipelago of overpriced appetizers covered their table: warm lobster salad with arugula, a mound of New Zealand mussels and wispy, golden fries.

"We have a model," one of them said. "It's the total dedication model. You can't go halfway. It's binary. You're either with us or against us."

Wayne wasn't sure what they were talking about but decided that whatever it was he was against them. He smiled smugly. For the first time she noticed that one of his teeth had a filling. He stood up and excused himself to the bathroom. She noticed his tummy; an all-too-human mound of fat hung around his waist. When he came back he looked bruised, as if he had been beaten. He had every reason to be happy. The Dow Jones Industrial Average had fallen off a cliff and Empiricus Kapital had surged another three percent. The firm's equity capital had, in less than a year, virtually doubled, yet Wayne was crestfallen.

"The mussels are terrible," he said. "Let's go somewhere else."

"You look a bit down. Bad day at work?"

What else could it be? Wasn't work all that Americans talked about? Work, work, work—and the size of their swimming pool. If this thought was critical it was because of her belief that in a material age there was more than matter to be trusted.

"I actually had a very good day," Wayne snapped back. "When the market is down, we make money. When it's up, we lose money. It was down today, so in theory, *I'm in the money*, except that I feel like crying."

It was not the sort of information one shared on a first date.

"What is it that you actually bet on?" she asked, feigning interest.

"Crisis," he said. "Revolution, recession, devaluation, bankruptcy, war, genocide, earthquake, natural and man-made disaster, coup d'etat, nuclear meltdown; anything that might send a country into the scrap heap of history. You name it, we'll trade it."

"Who for?"

"I can't share that with you."

"How big is the fund?"

"I can't share that with you."

A few seconds later he offered: "Let's just say if it had tits, the cup would be a size 42D.*

She considered landing a slap on his face, but remained

* French conversion results in a 130E. To date, there is no common European standard.

hopeful that he would recite a Shakespearean sonnet before the end of the night. As he haltingly reached for a mussel, Wayne felt an invisible hand write *I feel down* across his forehead in Helvetica, twenty-point typeface.

"So why are you down?" she asked.

"Is it that obvious?"

"Tell me, what's wrong?"

"I can't share that with you."

A few seconds later he offered: "The Basilica. I feel terrible."

The last thing she wanted to talk about was the Basilica bombing.

"Terrorism has made a comeback," he said. "It's no longer in beta."

2.

AS THE CONVERSATION turned to politics, Alix wondered if Wayne would ever ask her a question about herself. She had already prepared her answers. What was her birth sign? Sagittarius. Did she have unusual features on her body? A series of birthmarks on her belly in the shape of a vertical galaxy. How did she spend her days? Reading books, walking on the rooftops of buildings. What did she think of the United States? She was openly critical of it. She felt odd to be in a country where one's worth was determined by how much money one made. As a student, her monthly allowance amounted to no more than 1,050 euros. Did she like New York? Yes. No. Maybe. It was too soon to tell. It certainly felt like a city that was supremely confident in itself. And what was it like to live in Marseille? The pundits of good taste would say nothing but sloppiness and poverty. But there was always the sun and the sea. Had she ever tried a bouillabaisse? Yes, of course she had. She actually favored the bouillabaisse over the beluga, that is to say, the cult of quantity-over-scarcity value. She had prepared other coquette answers, patiently waiting for the questions that never arrived.

She considered Wayne: undertaxed and overworked. Across their table, a stiff man with red cheeks cut into a soft, pink steak. She recalled a philosophical observation that Roland Barthes had made: *To eat a steak rare was supposed to present both a nature and a morality.* She wondered if Wayne too presented a morality, or if he was simply unreachable, living in that guilt-free mathematical zone that was beyond good and evil. She wanted to make love to him before returning to Marseille. It was not out of philosophical compulsion that she felt this sudden urge. It was destined desire, self-willed, so that her mind had little control over it.

3.

THEY WALKED DOWN a deserted alley off Canal Street into Alonzo's Chinese Noodle Shop. It was one of the last vestiges of the Italians in this part of grubby New York. This place was a definite downgrade from SoHo, she thought. A yellow faux-marble wall featured a jade-green depiction of the Great Wall of China. There were three featherless ducks hanging from hooks over the chef's head. A dull, fluorescent light refracted into a fish tank. The room smelled of vegetable oil and pepperoni pizza. Contrary to the restaurant's name, noodles were absent from the menu. Wayne surveyed the prices, reading from right to left. Alix examined the aquarium, which was deserted except for a grumpy, tired fish that seemed to boycott its own existence. At the other end of the restaurant four men spoke Mandarin, negotiating their plastic chopsticks with blue bowls of rice. There was also a nerdy hipster in Noam Chomsky glasses, the consummate graduate student, sitting across from an attractive almost-model. And there was Alonzo, the irascible Italian chef who had hurled profanities at the constant influx of Chinese immigrants pouring into his turf. He stooped over a box of pizza in the kitchen. Alonzo's was a dumpy canteen, populist at its core, with plaster peeling from its yellow walls. It was the type of place that reminded one that prosperity in the world was expanding at a slower pace than the overall population.

"The morons changed the menu," Wayne said. "They have pizza and dumplings, but I don't see any noodles."

It was over a plate of steamed dumplings that he first apologized for having been a moron himself ever since they'd met. He confessed that he was actually very excited to see her. He meant to compliment her on her blue eyes, each the size of a two-euro coin, but hedged at the last minute, for fear that he was being too forward. He wanted to ask her many questions: her sign; if she had unusual features on her body; how she spent her days; if she liked New York; what it was like to live in Marseille; if she enjoyed writing her thesis; if she would consider going to a gallery opening with him the next day. All of these questions were at the tip of his tongue, until a cloud of anxiety descended on him. His poker face took an unexpected form, and his *esprit de guerre* turned softer than a Camembert.

During this uncertain moment in space and time the market was caught in the vortex of a downward spiral. And so with each passing second, the past expanded, compressing the future, but which future? Wayne knew the exact space-time coordinates of one of these futures.

4.

"WHAT IS IT LIKE TO LIVE in Marseille?" he finally asked while chewing on steamed bok choy. Before she could answer, Wayne's Nokia vibrated and he excused himself from the table.

"Put Marseille on hold for a second, I'll be right back."

At the other end of the phone was Brad Porcella, one of his traders who followed the Asian markets.

"Dude, headline risk is looking good in Korea," he said.

"Right," said Wayne, and they both hung up.

He returned to the table and shared the good news with Alix, a beaming smile on his face, wider than a junk bond spread.

"There is an exponential growth in despair in Korea beyond the historical standard of deviation," he said.

The first indications of this exponential growth in despair took the form of numbers. They made their way onto Bloomberg screens, a riot of never-ending, ever-changing fractions caught in an epileptic fit. It was as if the quantifiable world were shrinking. Stock valuations were sliced in half. Then North Korea issued a declaration in characteristic understatement: "We will strike back wherever there is sky, land or water. We will not let them leave the swamp *they* have entered. *They* will meet their fate."

It was not clear who *they* were referring to. One never knew with the mercurial half peninsula. Wayne called Porcella and instructed him to sell more futures into the weakness tomorrow.

"Mon pauvre bébé," she said, "just a minute ago it looked like you were carrying the entire world on your shoulders."

"I'm tired. It's been a trying week."

"If you're too tired to go out, just think how you'll feel at seventy-three. Live a little."

She put her chopsticks down and reached over the last dumpling. He felt a tingle in his vascular vessels. His heart came close to producing tears, one more twist and it would have, a gnarled, impregnable heart in need of compassion. He held her hand for the first time without thinking about the fate of global capitalism.

"Is everything okay?"

"Couldn't be better," he said, regaining his Delphic composure. "The dumplings are excellent."

5.

THE NEXT DAY ALIX and Wayne met at Tony Feher* on West Twenty-second. He tried to make sense of the ominous

* It's actually an art gallery.

title of the retrospective. It was called (W)holes and Boundaries: The Dictatorship of the Viewer. He had no idea what it meant, but owing to the postmodern theme he was confident that many New Age philosophers would attend. While browsing a promotional brochure, Alix came across the name of one of the organizers, Dr. Felix Maudin, a self-described "paradisciplinary French relativist moral philosopher, professor, architect, sculptor, writer, painter and documentary filmmaker."

Maudin arrived at the opening with a swarthy boy from Bangalore. There was little reason in what the boy wore: a rainbow-colored fez, a white Indian shirt, spandex tights and fluorescent Nikes. The boy looked traumatized, as if he had just converted to postmodernism. Maudin himself was dressed in ghetto fabulous. He carried a translucent neoprene briefcase with nothing inside. They took their time touring the gallery. They said *bonjour* to everybody. "Darling, please, I've seen better art hanging in the Lufthansa guest lounge," Maudin concluded. His was a perspective informed by a creative household: at an early age, he dressed up his toothbrush in little skirts he made.*

Alix surveyed the septic walls of the gallery. What the critics called art were random squiggles and lines masked as ironic detachment. She looked at one of the installations: a series of windows and viewing cones that captured disassembled plants, broken at the bract, mangled. There was the smell of chloro-

* *The New York Times*, "Tumbling From Hip-Hop Heights," by Lola Ogunnaike, September 21, 2003.

phyll in the air. She had seen many of these plants on sale in Marseille. They were everywhere. She had one in her studio. It sat on a sill, comfortably constant. She peered into one of the viewing cones. What had these plants done to deserve such a fate?

"As viewers, you're all oppressors," Maudin suddenly proclaimed to the crowd. "You inject your personal history into everything you look at. Not unlike a dictator who imposes his individual history onto society." His voice was high-pitched, mocking. When Alix finally approached Maudin, the postmodern groupies had formed a tight knot around him. They followed his words, swelling above the crowd like some kind of coded incantation. He talked about a bombing, or the art of bombing, or the bombing of art. It was difficult to tell what the postmodernists ever talked about.

"Darling, there is *nada.* No-thing. It's the end of Western hegemony, if not of dialectical history," he declared. "Forgive me for pooh-poohing your American administration, but I must take them to task for their appropriations, maneuvers, techniques and functionings, all of which, of course, should be examined in a network of relations, constantly in tension, in activity."

"I think we should go," Wayne said. "I can't take any more of this bullshit, plus there is no price list."

That night, when Alix entered Wayne's loft, she took note of the remarkable interior. There was the cement floor, the palindromic procession of Corbusier-inspired columns. She walked to the bathroom past a Haans Wegner original, somewhat critical of the bronze standing tub for which Wayne had paid $17,500 at a Sotheby's auction. It was clear to her that he was aiming for a purist composition in harmony with the classical canon.

"This is what I came up with," he said, opening up his arms to the loft like a conductor. "I handpicked all of the pieces."

Everything in his loft engendered proportion. Even the night had passed with relative equilibrium, an evening that had not been smashed under the mathematical sum of too many errors. In bed they held hands, which seemed a bit odd to him. At three in the morning he rolled off the mattress onto the *tatami,* propelled by an unknown force. He threw himself back on the mattress, searching for her hand. As he took stock of the day's events, her fingers twitched as if she inferred every wrinkle in his thinking.

"Are you awake?" she asked.

"What is it?"

"Just go to sleep."

"Stop waking me."

His voice, suspended in the darkness, prompted her to turn around, so that she pressed her behind against his, their hands still clasping uncomfortably. Wayne's neurological receptors went into overdrive, trying to make sense of the day's events. The fact that she was next to him meant little on its own. He rarely judged reality by its outcome or by what was happening to him in the present. He measured it by the costs of its alternative histories. It was only in the past few months that he began to look at the world this way. He took after his father, the bridge builder, who believed that matter was solid, and certainly her body pressing against him was proof of that. But even when her matter imposed itself upon him in the present, could it not, when broken down into atoms, evanesce into microscopic, invisible forms? Reality was complicated, multipolar, present, absent. It was in too many places at the same time.

"Are you asleep?" she asked again.

"I can't."

"What are you thinking about?"

"Your presence."

She wiggled against him. "What about it?"

"It's making me see the world in a different way."

"Take a closer look," she said, and took off her T-shirt.

He steered his index finger along her back, then gently pressed it into her atlas. So much converged there.

"Do you want to give me a *fessée*?"

"A what?"

"A provocative slap on my ass," she said pedagogically. "It's a French invention."

He gently tapped her right buttock.

"What was that?"

"I don't want to hurt you."

"No, no, no," she said. "Slap me harder. I want you to make it red. Express yourself."

6.

IT WAS STILL DARK OUTSIDE when Wayne got up to shower. He performed the same ablutions that he did every morning under the cold water. He washed his hair with lavender and aloe organics, tucked his tummy in and knelt in his bronze standing tub to pray to the gods of science. He had an investors' conference to attend at the Grand Hyatt on the future of wireless providers. He put his Perry Ellis shirt on, strapped a Carrera watch around his wrist, the first to combine split-second timing with instant legibility. He walked to the kitchen and opened the fridge, which was virtually empty except for a pair of kiwis from Whole Foods, a carton of nonbiologically modified soja milk, a bottle of San Pellegrino, a dozen quail eggs from Dean & DeLuca and two pots of Petrossian caviar. He scooped the shiny black eggs with a teaspoon, eating them like cereal. He turned the stove on and grabbed three quail eggs, breaking them against the circumference of the skillet.

"Is that the smell of coffee burning?" Alix asked from under the ruffled sheets.

"Just my mind going into overdrive."

"Whatever it is that you're cooking, I'll have half of."

"I'm out the door at five past four. Why don't we meet at Battery Park later? We can have a hot dog somewhere and I'll show you the boats in the harbor."

"Why are you going so early?"

"I have an investors' conference I need to do homework for. Make yourself at home. There is kiwi in the fridge, clean towels in the drawer."

"Merci, mon coeur."

He kissed her nose and ran out the door.

Wayne stepped into the cobblestone street in front of his building, and within five seconds there was a Yellow Cab in front of him. As he took his seat he looked at the driver's name plate: Jatin Singh. The last thing he needed to hear at four in the morning was a loquacious Indian cabby telling him that this was not his real vocation, that in Bangalore he was a respected mathematician researching the calculus of probability, that in his spare time (Sunday nights) he would stay holed up in his studio to finish a philosophical treatise on the geography of nowhere—wherever that was. Fortunately, the only comment from the driver referred to a directional shift to avoid a rooftop water tank explosion on West Broadway. Wayne felt particularly good today.

When he reached Empiricus, the doorman greeted him with a military salute.

"Good morning, Mr. Wayne."

"Morning, Mike."

"Did you hear? A water tank blew up near your building. I was worried about you," he said, worried, no doubt, about his year-end bonus.

"Thanks, but it was actually a few blocks away."

Kiss-ass, he thought, and it's not even five in the morning.

Wayne jumped into the elevator, eager to get a head start on the rest of New York. The city was still asleep and the streets were empty. Dunkin' Donuts would soon open across the street. He'd get a medium, maybe a large with milk on the side, before heading to the investors' conference.

As Wayne stepped into the office his cell phone rang.

"Empiricus Kapital."

"We're about to establish ecological balance," the voice at the other end said. "The future is green."

The line went dead before he could say anything. He was expecting the call, yet did not share the Corsican's view about a bucolic future. For him, the future was a place absent of color. The future was numerical. The future was a stochastic process, so that there were always independent developments occurring simultaneously in different geographic locations: if one area suffered a setback, another development would take its place in the same general time frame. Perhaps this was why there were so many alternate paths leading to the same destination, so that the future would take care of itself, like it always did.

Wayne put his Nokia away and turned on his computer. He turned his feelings off. During these early hours the office was eerily quiet except for the ambient chirps emanating from machines. He entered helios9 as the enabling password: an autobiographical reference to the city that never sleeps. The only source of light in the office came from the screensaver, featuring wraparound text: *We're Not Technology's Final Product,* it affirmed, then looped around the screen. Wayne appreciated the self-referential fatalism of the devices around him.

He stepped up to the wall of glass. His thoughts were lost in a forest of vertical celestials. He measured the scale of the buildings, wondering what was happening inside each one of them. He squinted his eyes and isolated a window on the surface of a building. He imagined that in the room two traders exchanged stories around an electric campfire. One of them told the story of the sound of lost money. "All you are left with is this silence in the office," he said, "and a dozen hedge fund guys staring at their red screens and you know that the fund is going to be wound down and everyone is thinking about whose fucking fault it is and how fast it happened, and you see all the hubris shrivel into wounded, worthless shame, and all that you're left with during the day, which never seems to end, is this unbearable silence of money being lost, tens of millions, and you find out after the close about another redemption from another one of the big investors and you feel sick in your stomach and walk out into the night from a Midtown tower still in a daze and you walk across Fifty-ninth Street past the Plaza, the park on one side and the smell of horse shit in the air, and then you notice a beggar, and as you walk past him he lets out a thunderous, ephemeral fart, which is also the sound of lost money."

Bunch of maggots, Wayne thought, it would never happen to him.

He returned to his Herman Miller desk and gave an affectionate tap to his loyal laptop, *ready-prompt* for some data mining. Next, he moved to the petty task of deleting email. The most obnoxious came from Brett Fortunoff, another PM* from a rival hedge fund under the subject heading of *coopetition. Coopetish* what? Wayne scratched his head. Doesn't anyone speak English anymore?

In the spirit of cooperative competition we remain open to sharing our research with Empiricus Kapital and eventually opening the way to a synergetic merger of our assets under joint management.

Wayne, however, was interested in economies of time, not scale. Time was the dimension out of which all other dimensions emerged. It pressed against every space, every corner, every edge. He wondered how long it would take to move his finger to the delete key. No more than a second. Moments later he Googled "Empiricus Kapital." One of the links led to a certain Jayanti Pinchu, an investor advisor in Kuala Lumpur, who posted the following message in a public forum:

Given continued uncertainty in the Asian markets, stick with Empiricus Kapital. They continue to do well in a difficult global environment.

* Portfolio Manager.

The second link led to an anonymous message on a financial thread. It may have been nothing more than a canard concocted by a jealous rival. The poster accused Wayne of bad behavior as he lunched one day at the Odeon. The charge? That he bought options on his neighbor's asparagus, then stood up and pulled his pants down. The image of Carl Icahn was displayed across the backside of his boxers. Rumors. They are not to be believed. They are there to be denied, or, if the market is open, to be traded on. The last link led to an error message from the systems administrator, for which Wayne remained cautiously optimistic. If anyone accused him of wrongdoing there was little proof of it. The world or at least the World Wide Web stood as witness.

As the sun stretched over Manhattan, Wayne opened his desk drawer and pulled out a tattered copy of Marx's *Capital.* He flipped to chapter six, "Buying and Selling of Labor-Power." He read several pages every morning, more out of idle curiosity than ideological conviction. Sometimes he smiled a deprecating smile when he came across a vitriolic, self-righteous passage. If his reading was glib—and it was true, he often skipped over the more headache-inducing pages—it was because his foremost allegiance was to money. Fungible money. Transnational money. One could never have enough of it. It was hard work chasing money. It had taken him more than four years to make his first $40 million.

But it wasn't just about money. Was Marx completely oblivious to a world beyond matter? When he made love to Alix, Wayne had stopped to think that he was the sum of his labor. He had emotions too, and this was of historical consequence.

After reading several pages he wanted to leave the office and head back to the loft. He wanted to slip under the bedsheets next to her and count the beauty marks on her back.* He wanted to embrace her. He wanted to take her pulse but resisted this impulse. He kept on reading: "In order to modify the human organism so that it may acquire skill and handiness in a given branch of industry and become labor-power of a special kind, a special education or training is requisite." And what were the core competences of a short-seller, beyond a cold, rational commitment to bet against the consensus?

By seven a.m. there were too many questions racing through his head. As team Empiricus trickled in, Wayne slipped out the door. He crossed the street to Dunkin' Donuts for a regular. He walked briskly. He passed a shiny infotainment store and a knot of Asian tourists heading in the direction of the Grand Hyatt. He arrived at the conference hall an hour early, scouring the grounds for promotional freebies. He grabbed a Cable & Wireless logo hat with a pewter buckle. He stuffed it into a Nokia messenger bag, with adjustable nylon web straps. He sampled a selection of next-generation handhelds. The most fascinating was a typhoon phone-watch portable that displayed tide information for 175 surfing beaches around the world.

* Different than birthmarks mentioned on page 77.

That's fucking awesome, dude.

He threw one in his shopping bag, which was weighed down by many other futuristic prototypes so that he had difficulty carrying it. He then walked over to a Bloomberg terminal. There was a technology butler next to the machine, a hotel staffer to help investors with stupid questions. He entered the symbol for the Bustaci Frères Fiber Company and for a moment he thought of the Corsican. Having filed for bankruptcy, the company no longer traded on the global exchanges, but many of its employees were now working for *him.* Several were in Spain taking measurements of Calatrava's bridges; others were in Russia, Japan, the U.S. and the U.K. He then looked at the leading stock markets of the world. They were all down. The Vix* trended higher. Before he left the Hyatt he took a bite into a complimentary pretzel, hubris in his heart, a big swinging dick in his Bernini trousers.

Truth be told, it was his interest in architecture and not the size of his penis that touched her. He knew about bridges. He knew about the Basilica. He knew about the plinth that Mies used to elevate his structures above the earth. As she crossed Canal, a familiar hip-hop beat blared from a car stereo. It was Bad Boy: *Mase got the ladies, Puff drives Mercedez.* She wanted to throw her hands up in the air and wave them like she didn't care.

* Known on Wall Street as the fear gauge.

When she reached Battery Park, Wayne was still at Empiricus, brushing his teeth in the bathroom. She toured the docks on her own, taking note of the recreational boat names: *Escape, Liquid Asset, Wet Dream, Predator.*

7.

IN THE OFFICE BATHROOM, Wayne washed his face with a green exfoliating scrub. He put his Ralph Lauren glasses on, took off his work shirt, smelled his armpits and put it back on again. He was anxious to see her. But first he entered one of the stalls. He pulled his pants down and crouched on the toilet. He squinted his eyes at the white electric spark in the neon tubing above him. Then his neighbor from Seneca Capital walked in. He recognized Wayne's hand-crafted Varda shoes from under the stalls and took the one next to him. He pulled his pants down and crouched on the toilet. The most striking attributes about the Seneca money manager were that he was from Georgia and that he spoke in a loud voice. Today the manager was on the verge of tears, having lost the fund's capital in a series of poorly conceived trades. His colleagues wanted to strangle him, especially those in Research, whose advice he never followed. And now he would have to pay the price. He was going to be fired. It was only a matter of time, the only truly scarce commodity.

"Hiya," he said. "This market is killin' me. It's a fuckin' freak show out there." He laid on a thick accent at first as an affirmation of his primary identity, reverting to a more neutral tone, the acquired language of universal money.

"Sure is," Wayne said, more in moral support than in actual belief. "So what's your take on the market *arb,* man?"

"If you asked me last week, I was sittin' pretty as a pup, then it kept comin' at me like stink on shit. Maybe Marx was right," he said with cynical derision. "Maybe the victory of the proletariat is inevitable."

"Tough week last week."

"Sure fuckin' was. I'm not askin' for much, just wanna break even."

"You can't break even," Wayne said. "Don't you remember from physics class? It's impossible to return to the same energy state. There is always an increase in disorder. Entropy always increases."

"Give me a break, man. I've had enough of your theory of deterministic disaster. I don't need to be lectured."

There was silence for several seconds, followed by intestinal rumbling, then a thunderclap in the stall. In order for us to know that something is there we must first bump into it, Wayne reflected in a moment of abstraction.

He gathered his thoughts and offered some words of support: "Hey, man, don't feel down: Soft. Strong. Lasts Long." It was a marketing slogan from Scott Paper, which cost less per sheet than other national rivals. The Georgian felt particularly attached to the white unscented, having made a fortune and a name for himself when he bought the stock as a young, indomitable trader.

"So how are you holding?" Wayne asked.

"Diarrhea. We're down eight percent for the year. I can't get out of most of my stock, and of course there are the options. But they can all go to pot, I'm prepared for it."

"Take 'em off. Get rid of 'em."

"Too late for that, I'm zapped. I'm about to get fired, my wife is threatenin' me with divorce and I need reconstructive knee surgery. I've managed to lose all we have—the farm, the house, the two cars, the boat. I mean, Wayne, you know, we weren't rich as Huguenots, but we had everythin' we needed, which I'm ashamed to say I'm now divestin' for extra money."

Wayne flushed the toilet, eager to leave; enough of this maudlin confessional. "Serious shit goin' on everywhere," he said. "You should have listened to me when I told you that the market was weak. Anyway, all of this—the market, the Fed, the payroll numbers—it's all fucking bullshit."

"Fuckin' bullshit is right. I should have gone short the SPYs, but the economy seemed row-bust and inflation was tame and Ben Bernanke seemed like he knew what he was sayin', so I backed up the truck, and then outta nowhere, zap!"

"That fucking Bernanke, he's fuck," Wayne interjected. "People follow his words like he's the Messiah, and maybe he is, but last week was the week you should have bet on the side of the Antichrist."

"Easy to say in hindsight. I just don't fuckin' know anymore. Anyway, I took the plunge and we bought into two types of funds, one an index of government bonds, the other a basket of growth stocks. The bonds are doin' fine, but the stocks are killin' me, slipperier than a greased pig at a pork roast."

"What about your other holdings?"

"Bunch of clunkers I can't get out of."

"If it's any consolation, you're not the only one having a soft year."

"That's what I keep tellin' myself, that we're all in a difficult environment. But it doesn't mean that they should have humiliated me the way they did. Look at this memo Research sent me. I got it this mornin.'" And with that, the money manager from Seneca slipped the memo to Wayne from under the stall.

Some Trading Rules to Live By
An Intra-Office Memo from Seneca Capital

1. To gain control you must be prepared to lose control
   there was a time not long ago when you were on a roll.

2. Most of the market is non-linear in the same way that most of zoology is non-zebra
   how does it feel to be an ex–money manager from the state of Georgia?

3. Predictability is short-term just like the weather
who just dumped all those shares of your favorite bellwether?

4. Small causes could have large effects, prompting the entire market to become unstable
you might as well hide under the table.

5. If you don't sell now it's not a loss
until the margin clerk reminds you who's the boss.

"Hang in there," Wayne said. "I'd love to talk more, but I'm running late." He flushed the toilet and ran out. He took the elevator down and gave a salute to the doorman.

"Good day, chief?"

"Good day, Mike."

Another win-win day at Empiricus Kapital.

He took a large stride into Fifty-sixth Street, almost stepping over a poodle, until their paths diverged and he hurled himself into the first Yellow Cab, slamming the door behind him. A steely voice greeted him from the speakers:

"This is Clint Eastwood, reminding you to buckle up for safety."

"Battery Park," he said, buckling up not just for safety but for Darwinian survival. "If we get there inside fifteen minutes, this is yours." He waved a hundred-dollar bill in the air. If there was any hint of causality between this prodigal offer and the car's velocity, it quickly fell apart to the rush-hour traffic. It would take at least twenty minutes to reach their destination, even if the driver managed to shave off a minute or two—at the margin. "God is great," said Mahmoud the driver. "I will be trying to put the metal to the pedal."

"Lock and load," Wayne said. "Let's rock 'n' roll."

When he finally found her she was sitting on a mound of grass, eating a burrito, thinking about the last few days. There was a grape-colored reduced-sugar beverage in a recycled bottle next to her, a cool calorie-conscious drink to quench her thirst. She was feeling tired and wanted to take a cab back to the loft. She had already spent an hour at Gourmet Garage, walking past the never-ending display of designer food in all kinds of non-Euclidian combinations that stretched the linear frontiers of her epicurean imagination. She was brought up eating simple things that came out of predictable tins and boxes. Where did all of this food come from? Who prepared it? Were the prices simply a question of supply and demand? Where was the excess food stored at the end of the day? The onion rye bread with Scottish malt syrup, the morel mushroom toasts, the king salmon in fig leaves, the country terrine with Tunisian pistachios, the warm lamb salad with pomegranates and walnuts, the duck confit with baked figs, the pan-fried truffled chicken breasts, the sour cream crab enchiladas, the pizzeta with farm egg and prosciutto, the pan-fried stuffed squash bottoms, the gravlax and cucumber salad, the shaved parmesan asparagus salad, the cherry clafoutis, the chocolate espresso custard, the shiatsu cookies, the baked bananas in port, the almond torte, all of it sold against a background of classical music in a genial atmosphere tempered by that egalitarian public good that was the air conditioner, available to everyone for free.

"So you had a good day?"

"Sort of."

"What's wrong?"

"You're going to think that I sound like a little girl in a floral dress, but I keep thinking of the Basilica bombing," she said. "Who would do such a thing?"

"I'm not sure you should pursue that line of questioning," Wayne said. "Why don't we walk up to Elizabeth Street and talk about something else?"

"I'm a little tired. Can we go back to your place?"

"Let's do it."

And they did. Twice during the course of the night, the most memorable of which involved the Hans Wegner chair made of leather and steel. She was hesitant at first.

"Your chair is like a *liturgique* object," she said. "You think I would dare put my bottom on it?"

But she eventually did.

"May it be divine."

He pulled his pants down and embraced her.

"Mon cher bébé, cheri d'amour," she said, and recoiled her thighs on the steel armrests. When he made love to her she whispered a list of requests and affirmations. Then she asked him to stop for a moment. She walked over to the kitchen for a

glass of water, after which they climbed back into bed kissing. She would leave him soon, leaving behind her smell lingering on his mattress, his lips on her imaginary hips, her particles on his heavy coat. Next week he would find a hair strand on one of his shirts like a thread of gossamer, the filament of a lonely lightbulb illuminating the darkest precincts of his imagination. He would feel her inside of him, racing through his intestinal tract with Herculean strides.

"I wish I could stay longer," she said.

"Me too."

"I think of you."

"I think of you too."

"Je t'embrasse. Tes yeux, ton téton droit, ton sexe, ton coeur, ta voix."

"I think therefore I am *with you.*"

"Whatever," she said. "Can't you come up with something more original?"

"It's a play on Descartes," he said. "I was taking it a step further."

"I know about Descartes," she said. "He was a lousy lover."

It was then that he noticed her sleepy left eye. It drooped to one side like a tired sunset signaling the end of the day. Inside her iris he could see the ultraviolet rays of a solar star. This reminded him of his first love, Elizabeth Malkovitch, who suffered from a similar condition.

"You have a sleepy eye," he said.

"I feel sleepy."

"Look at me."

"I am. You look at me."

"I am."

"No, you're not."

"Yes, I am."

"My eye in your eye," she said.

"You're worth a million dollars," he said.

"Is that all?"

8.

WAYNE FELT UNEASY ABOUT his good fortune in the market. What joy was there in making money from the misery of the planet? At least he had her emails to look forward to after she left. He went into his inbox to see if she had written to him. The market was about to open. For the first time in many years he did not care about the numbers. He did not care if Nasdaq opened flat, if it gapped up or if it spent the entire day trading sideways. There was an FOMC meeting later in the day. He waited for hours for the anticipated reduction in the overnight rate. When the Fed dropped rates, he yawned. He fell into a lull. She finally sent him an email. He dug into it like an archaeologist. He flipped each word upside down, searching for clues into the hidden meta-language of her mind. What would he find there? Steel pipe structures, maybe, or the buckling load of an isotropic sphere, a mesh of almost equilateral triangles, layers of pipes tied by bridles, elastic instabilities, the meridians and parallels of a dome, perhaps, the ponding of a flat roof following water accumulation.

The day after she returned to Marseille she skipped her engineering class. Her mind was far from the finer points of force and form. She enjoyed answering his questions about wide-angled steel beams, but did he really care about her?

"Mon cher gros bébé cheri," she wrote. *"Je rentre d'un epuisante journée.* I'm not sure when we'll meet again, but when we do, I'd like you to plant more planets inside of me. Please let me know about you and never forget, I am on your side, thinking of you. Alix des Baux."

To which Wayne responded with budding signs of sentiment (while the stock market traded sideways):

Roses are red,
Violets are blue,
I keep rolling in my bed
Thinking of you.
There is this alkaloid girl,
Her name is Alix,
She is my little pearl
Lost in the tropics.

Her left eye is sleepy,
For some it may be creepy,
But I like the distance
Between her pupil and mine.
Roses are red,
Violets are blue,
The stock market is dead
And I Dove you too.

Minutes later, while he was selling Icelandic bonds, an Instant Message popped up on his screen. "For a second I confused your poem for one of Frédéric Mistral's. Have you thought about giving up stock trading and considered a career as poet?"

"Let me get back to you on that," he wrote back. "By the way, who is Alix des Baux?"

"She was the last princess of Les Baux de Provence, a village of staggering beauty perched on a limestone cliff, where my parents once made love in an abandoned windmill."

"That's sweet. I'd love to IM with you, but my Bloomberg beckons and I'm anticipating a run on the Icelandic krona."

"What is it with these islands and financial meltdown? Go back to work, just want you to know that I was thinking of you the other day while languishing in my bed and all of a sudden an angel plum plunged into my hair and I almost thought it was some kind of grace attack."

9.

When they met again, the Corsican nearly had a heart attack. A sharp pain penetrated his chest as he watched her walk into the hotel. They walked along the periphery of the harbor as they habitually did and settled on the second-floor balcony of the Caravelle. The harbor bustled with the mad rush of people dispersed in a multitude of directions. The anchored boats creaked and groaned as if suffering from a chronic arthritic condition. The summer light descended on the Notre Dame de la Garde perched on top of a hill facing their table. The cathedral basked in the glory of the afternoon sun. It was a majestic and uncomplicated view, yet for the Corsican it was no more than a marketing image, fundamentally spectacular by nature, a visual representation that aimed at nothing other than itself. He wondered how many tourists climbed up the hill today to take a closer look at the cathedral, this hallowed confusion, which to him was a material reconstruction of the religious illusion.* It was no different with the Basilica di San Marco, to which he did not feel any particular attachment either. His god was made of wood and grass. She was made of water and detritus and red ants and there was no other god to which he would surrender. He thought of the postcards the gift

* From "The Society of Spectacle," by Guy Debord.

shops at such places sold, the captivating portraits of cathedrals, pyramids, churches and mosques frozen under the sun; a sun that never set over the empire of illusion.

He looked at her sublime features. He wanted to kiss her but was afraid that she would turn her face away in the direction of the cathedral. She was the fairest of all the women he had known. Her only flaw was that she had not been born on an island. She smelled of many things to him: the deepest was of Provence, the damp smell of fishermen wrestling with wet fish. She smelled of the ancient abbey of Fontfroide and of the silent unruffled sky. She smelled of loamy fields and of inverted oceans and of particles, coarser than clay, when buildings fell down. And then a violent impulse raced through him. When she told him that she would leave him he thought of pushing her off the balcony. It was a vague desire, nothing to worry about. She spoke with an air of ennui, staring at the islands of tapas on the table, the plates of wrinkled olives, bits of octopus and stacks of sardines. The pain grew in his chest and he thought of walking away, putting the matter to rest. Now his eyes began to swell and he tried to think of something cheerful to hold back his tears. He remembered the first occasion of their meeting at the hotel where she had gone to pick up a copy of the *Tribune*. He was sitting at the bar when he first saw her. The Corsican asked if she was English or American. But I am French, she said, can't you see, I haven't given up on smoking. This made him laugh and later on they had their first conversation at the bar. The Corsican told her why he was in Marseille.

It was to set up a maquis in the Vosges. They were going to call this camp New Babylon. It was going to be a camp in the middle of nature designed by a Dutch architect in his group whose name was Constant and he was putting the finishing touches on a text called *For an Architecture of Situation.* Did she want to see it? Yes, of course she did. She too was going to be an architect. They decided to meet again and this time he recounted the socio-agrarian makeup of New Babylon. It would eventually transform into a military camp and from there spread out over the whole country. They were going to derail trains. "But the army and the police," she protested. "You aren't sure of having the support of the population. You're precipitating a catastrophe."* The plan to build a camp in the Vosges was eventually abandoned and Alix never met the other members of the group. She agreed to pass along her sketches to the Corsican only because she enjoyed spending time with him. And now she had forgotten to bring her drawings for a second week. He would not have made much of this if he had not received the very same drawings from Wayne. At the bottom of each were her initials and many of the sketches were of buildings they had talked about at the hotel.

"You look upset," she said.

"I'm upset at the world."

"We have to move on."

"I'm not upset at you."

* From *October 79.* Interview with Henri Lefebvre of Situationist International, by Kristin Ross.

And then he told her about his next spectacle, a Situ event in the interior of the island. Did she want to participate? Before she could say anything her phone vibrated on the table. It was a text message from Wayne:

"I've been having difficulty following the market ever since you left. I'd like to see you again, Wayne."

Alix smiled and excused herself from the conversation. She pressed the tiny keys on her tri-band. The source of the Corsican's pain was at the core of his heart and it now grew sharper, disintegrating the parcels of hope and reason in his body. He felt fragmented and more alone than ever.

"Sorry," she said, "it's just a message from a friend. I'll be done in a second."

"A good friend?"

"A good friend."

"A good foreign friend?"

"I'm not sure you need to know," she said. "Tell me more about the spectacle."

He did not say anything. It was humiliating to be thwarted by such ambivalence. On their way back to the hotel, Alix told him that she had another school project to work on. She gave him a hug and a smile. "Don't be a stranger," she said. He was not planning to be. She hurried to her apartment without making a stop at the *salon de thé.* Walking briskly through an alley, she took in the heady warmth of a bakery. Three boys ran down Rue d'Aubagne on their way to the football stadium. One was black, the others white and brown. They chanted,

"*Allez l'OM, allez!*" in unison. "*On craint* dégun!"* When she reached home she sent another calculated provocation his way: "Hey, cowboy, I just made love to you touching myself. Did you hear me moan?"

To which Wayne responded, a hurricane of heat in his loins, because of a weight-lifting injury at the gym:

"Have you been following the news? There was a bombing by a pro-nature group determined to redefine the relationship between architecture, urbanism and nature. They offered some vague comments about 'the limitations of existing urban paradigms . . . the ambiguity of the modern experience as captured by the skyscraper.' They want to do away with it. It's been another stressful week at the office. We're working on Sundays now. I really need a vacation."

His invitation for a holiday came unexpectedly from the Corsican. Concerned about the safety of electronic fund transfers, he asked Wayne to meet him in Marseille to deliver the money for the next spectacle. The notes were to be divided between dollar, euro and yen. Wayne appreciated the meticulous care with which the Corsican approached their project. He too had come a long way from being a naive high school student. Over the years he made the necessary adjustments artfully so that by his senior year his classmates called him Gecko. Said one of his

* Not afraid of *anyone*.

teachers in the school yearbook: "If you put cunning and chutzpah together, you get Wayne."

10.

CURRENCY FLUCTUATIONS WERE an unnecessary complication of floating exchange regimes that Alix did not pay attention to. Her friends had told her about how expensive life in New York was before she embarked on her trip, but when she'd gotten there, she realized that there were many exceptions to what they had said. The first sign had come at the airport when she'd sold one hundred euros in exchange for many more dollars and later on when she'd bought a bag of Haribo candy, which cost less in the United States. Later on Wayne had explained to her the principle of purchasing power parity, from which she'd looked away with a yawn.

While she welcomed the market's volatility in favor of the euro, she did not enjoy the sudden fluctuations in the Corsican's emotions. They moved in wild and unpredictable ways, but she still had respect for him, even if she could no longer follow him, and so she agreed to go out with him one last time when he called.

"Let's do it for old times' sake," he said. "I'm in Marseille for one night and my grandmother sends you her kisses and she also sends you a pork sausage from the butcher Martinetti."

"Okay," she said, "but I can't stay long."

That night they met at a concert at Espace Julien. Inside the hall, teenagers danced in epileptic fits, their T-shirts macerated in alcohol and sweat. Onstage was Fonky Fatimah, the diva of a local hip-hop quartet. Alix made her way through the crowd following Fatimah's lugubrious ballads. When Fatimah sang her anguished anthem "Camus Comatose," Alix felt a growing transgression around her. Among the clubbers was a civil servant from Paris who approached her. He wore a white T-shirt that bore a 1956 quotation that railed against colonialism: *"Privilégier la Corrèze plutôt que le Zambèze."* It was a call for the French government to stop spending money on foreign conquests at the expense of underdeveloped national regions. He had a vacuous face and a tattoo on his forearm. She could not make out if the tattoo was permanent or fade-away dye. In the twenty-first century, even a commitment to cool was transitory. He offered her a cool pastis, carefully folding the receipt in his wallet. It was not easy being a functionary.

The Corsican stood next to Alix, his temper rising with each passing second.

"What brings you to Marseille?" she finally asked the bureaucrat, upon hearing his pointy accent.

"Field observation," he said. "We're measuring the rate of

buildings falling down and their impact on the equity markets, the CAC 40 in particular. We're looking at establishing correlation, but I don't want to bore you with that."

He just wanted a blow job to forget his day job.

"Do you have a tattoo?" he asked, taking a sip of his *prunelle.* It was his best effort yet to be a rebel. Just at that moment the Corsican interjected.

"There is no correlation," he said. "There are buildings falling down and there are markets falling down. It's not that complicated, really."

"That's what we're looking into," the functionary said. "And what do you do for a living besides meddling into other peoples' conversations?"

"I fuck bureaucrats like you," the Corsican said, and punched his face.

He then grabbed his bloodstained Agnès b. T-shirt for which the functionary had paid 115 euros and pulled him in. There was the smell of dusty journals in the civil servant's hair and the Corsican wondered if he had read Max Weber. Then he felt Alix pull at his arm and he let go of him.

"T'es fou," she said, *"complètement dingue."*

They made their way through the thick crowd for the exit. They ran for several minutes down the steps to Rue d'Aubagne, descending onto the port. Clasping her hand, the Corsican spat obscenities into the night air.

"He just offered me a drink," Alix said, panting. "Why did you do that?"

"You should know that," the Corsican said. "Never, never ask me that."

"I appreciate that, *mon p'tit Napoleon,* but I really could do without the drama. I've already told you about how I feel about the whole situation."

When they reached the hotel he gave her a hug and a smile.

"Don't be a stranger," she said. "Are you going to be all right?"

He leaned toward her and once again she turned her face away in the direction of the cathedral. He was left alone with a sausage from Martinetti and his ignoble depredations.

"I forgot the sausage," he said, "it's up in my room."

"It's okay," she said. "You'll give it to me next time."

He stood in front of the Bellevue staring at the boats in the harbor. The lights from the surrounding shops melted on the dark surface of the water, milky and distorted reflections. They looked so tired they were going to sink. There were weary travelers finishing up their late-night meals before returning to their rooms. There were the truculent rough sailors from the Porte Autonome drinking their last pints of beer. He walked slowly to the edge of the harbor. There was a *pointu* not far from him, a small fisherman's boat, which reminded him of his father's dory made of acacia wood and sheets of plywood. He fished with him during their winter vacations when the water was cold and the island was free of tourists from the Continent. He remembered that awful day when the phone rang. It was early in the morning and everyone was asleep and he was the first to wake up. It was his uncle, who told him that something had happened to his father. Was he going to be all right? The uncle did not answer. How serious was it? The uncle's voice quavered. Father Grimaldi had gone fishing early that morning and never came back. It was the hand of beneficent nature that washed bits of the boat back to the shores of the island during that foggy day. But it was not nature that was responsible for his death. It was the Swedish commercial vessel, *Osbur,* carrying Geox* Italian shoes made in China. When Father Grimaldi was trampled under the weight of global capitalism the Corsican vowed that one day he would consecrate a special spectacle in his honor. He walked up to his room and fell asleep. When he woke up Wednesday at noon it was to the sound of a siren.

On her way back home, Alix stopped in front of a housing project. She entered the lobby, took the elevator to the roof and walked along the edge of the building. She stared at the black sea in the distance. There were flickering red and white lights along the periphery of a fishing village called l'Estaque. It was a silent moment that all of a sudden succumbed to the sonic boom of a jet fighter, somewhere above the Mediterranean. A tide unhinged from its center of gravity. A seagull screeched. A pelican popped to the surface of the water, rising into the night above

* The shoe that breathes.

the fishermen and their huge walls of webbing. The waves were determined to bury their dead, to bring the fish back into the fold, into the darkness beneath. Or perhaps they just wanted to kill. There was no time to remain still.

She took the elevator down. By the time she made it back to her studio it was two in the morning. She wanted to check her email, but not before a late-night snack. She walked to the kitchen and grabbed a bag of Haribo. She tossed a yellow bear into her mouth, followed by a red one. Her tongue twisted left and right. There was tempest in her mouth, terror in her teeth. As she condemned the bears to consumption she walked to the bathroom and stared into the mirror. She looked for the birthmark above her upper lip, the one that Wayne considered the day she left New York. It was tinier than a pinhead: a golden galactic speck, a spectacular splash of stardust, "an unexpected outlier with no causative explanation," he said. She was touched by his attention to detail, by the geometry of his confined imagination, trapped by interconnected points of desire ready to break out. She wondered if she was nothing more than measured seduction to him, a multitude of equidistant meanings, a composite of Pythagorean forms, of perfect parabolas and symmetrical spheres.

She kept staring into the mirror thinking of his loft in New York. It was functional and empty, except for the requisite designer pieces, a compendium of minimal modern comfort: the pliable plastic bookcase inspired more by itself than by the ideas that it held, the inescapably tortured *tatami* (if she ever moved in with him, a queen-sized bed would have to take its place); the Hans Wegner chair on which they had made love; the Ingo Maurer lamp whose fragile, linear frame suggested a home absent of children. The floor was cement gray in tribute to the workday. And what about her studio? It was only slightly larger than a prison cell: twenty-five square meters of IKEA hell, an incomplete sketch of the Richard Rogers Glasgow bridge on a peeling wall; a hand-woven Hakebo basket next to the entrance with Plantu the plant inside, standing tall. There were piles of books everywhere, totems to accumulated and well-ordered knowledge. She had no money for luxury. Yet she rarely let the size of her budget influence the size of her dreams. She washed her face with Saugella. She brushed her teeth with a microfine-bristled toothbrush. She used Aquafresh toothpaste: a patriotic swirl of blue, white and red condensed into a convenient tube. She walked back to her desk and powered her laptop. She connected to the World Wide Web, the spectacular globe at her fingertips. There was no email from Wayne, just some spam from a debt consolidation company. She threw herself on her bed feeling down, her index finger pressed against the birthmark above her lip.

She wrote to him in the morning:

"I keep thinking of New York, of that night we spent in Chinatown, the neon lights, the people in the streets, the clouds, the oysters, the stinking fish and you. I'd like to see you."

"Good, I'm getting bored here," he wrote back, "I've been reading the *Journal of Behavioral Finance* all day. I've been reading Nassim Taleb on the virtues of asymmetric payoffs. I've been reading Alan Abelson in *Barron's.* They're both good guys. But the other headlines make me sick: Payrolls Up, Unemployment Claims Down, Consumer Confidence Up, Inflation Down. I just want to get away from it all and hug you."

And when one day as he looked in disbelief at a tightening yield spread, an IM from her took his worries away.

"When are you going to send me another poem?"

"I thought you'd never ask," he wrote after spending two days on the following effort:

Roses are red,
Violets are blue,
I am full of dread
In spite of a coup.
You are on my mind,
I will never forget you.
The market is so unkind,
My riches overdue.
I hear the sound of money
Sloshing in my head.
I look at the screen,
My positions are dead. .
Roses are red,
Violets are blue,
Wish I were there,
Sitting next to you.

"PS. I am about to buy my ticket to Marseille. I fly into Marignane two weeks from today. I want to make reservations at the Unité, that ugly modernist building made of cement."

To which Alix responded:

"I know it well. I've been to the roof terrace many times. The steel bars are eating into the cement, but it still commands a lot of charm. The pillars on which it stands have a certain brutal lyricism to them. It's a linear structure, part of the International School. I am personally in favor of it."

The Merchant of Light

1.

WAYNE BOUGHT HIS TICKET from Orbitz.com, the third largest online travel site based on gross bookings. He then redirected his Web browser to Amazon.com and ordered a copy of *The Rough Guide to Provence & the Côte d'Azur.* At noon he walked over to Chase Manhattan* on Park and asked his account supervisor, Betty Johnson, to prepare 1.2 million in euro, dollar and yen, just as the Corsican had requested.

Before he returned to the MetLife Building he treated himself to tea and biscuits at Fauchon. The day progressed as expected until he took a bite into his avocado sandwich. He went ballistic. Once again, they had forgotten to include the avocado.

* Now JP Morgan Chase.

He was reminded of Heisenberg's uncertainty principle, in which even an avocado sandwich lacked its predictable defining feature. In place of the green fruit he sank his teeth into an empty atom. "Where is the avocado?" he yelled at the office intern, a newly minted MBA from Columbia. "Are you a fucking moron or what?"

"I'm sorry?"

"Avocado," he said. "A-V-O-C-A-D-O. Don't they teach you how to spell at Columbia? Let me ask you another question." He longed for the certainty of a Newtonian axiom. What goes up must come down. It no longer applied. Everything around him was in flux, in unregulated gyrating motion. He wanted to scream, a Munch-like *Scream,* full of pain and horror.

"Can an avocado be and not be in an avocado sandwich at the same time?"

"What?"

"Are you deaf? CAN AN AVOCADO BE AND NOT BE IN AN AVOCADO SANDWICH AT THE SAME TIME?"

"Uh, no."

"WRONG! What the fuck do they teach you at Columbia? The market? Math? Ethics? Useless tools. If you knew anything about Schrödinger's cat, you would have said yes and you would have been right."

"Whose cat?"

"Schrödinger's, moron. He came up with a fundamental postulate of quantum physics that two things can occupy the same place at the exact same time and therefore something can be and not be at the exact same time. Demonstrated by Schrödinger through a thought experiment that placed a cat in a lead box together with a radioactive atom and a flask of cyanide. If the atom decayed, and the Geiger counter detected an alpha particle, a hammer would break the flask, thereby killing the cat. But if the atom does not decay, the cat is alive. How do you know if it's dead or alive? You don't, since you can't see what's happening inside the box. If you had known that, maybe, just maybe, you would have hope of becoming someone, you little shit."

"I see," the intern said sheepishly. "So you still want me to get you an avocado?"

"Here's a dollar," Wayne said. "Get me two. And keep the change. I'm feeling lucky today."

It was a lie that he wore with increasing discomfort. He loosened his tie and unbuttoned his collar. Beads of cold sweat covered his forehead. He stretched his trembling arms to unlock the pain in his chest, the silent scream still trapped inside him. He put the sandwich aside and stared into the Bloomberg. There was bad news in Russia, which was good news for Wayne, but was it going to be enough? A virulent strain of hepatitis had broken out in Moscow and it was spreading like the plague by sewage-contaminated water.

"Jackpot!" Wayne yelled. "Outbreak, outbreak. Hepatitis is back!"

A few more keystrokes and an index of Russian sovereign bonds appeared on his screen. Before the close, they bounced off their intraday lows, resurgent. Wayne pounded his fist on the keyboard. Another headline appeared on the screen, a petrochemical tank explosion in Martigues. The CAC 40 didn't seem to notice. He suspected that an outside force was manipulating the market. It was not just greed or hubris that clouded his thinking; it was a growing uncertainty that he woke to every morning. It was easy to ascribe reason to events after they happened, but could anyone ever ascribe true meaning with certainty? He picked up his handheld and called the Corsican. Ever since his visit to New York the Corsican had sent him many architectural sketches. Among the drawings were technical notes concerning Santiago Calatrava's bridges. There was a printout of the Campo Volantin in Bilbao. There was a drawing of the Alamillo in Seville with details of the cables on the anchored side of the pylon. He had also sent him an essay on inclined secondary diagonals and a feasibility study outlining the restoration of a historic monument in Tokyo.

At the other end of the phone was the Corsican's trusty lieutenant, the curmudgeonly Figolu. He handed the phone to the Corsican, who wondered more about Alix's location than Wayne's. Could she be in New York at this very minute sleeping at his side?

"All my positions are underwater," Wayne said. "Can you give me something with scale?"

"I would much rather have a philosophical discussion," the Corsican said.

"Shoot," Wayne responded, "and don't be angry with me, dude, we're both on the same side of the same trade."

"The only trade I'm on the side of is light," the Corsican offered cryptically.

"Just tell me something: how do you value light? I mean, like, there is so much of it already. How do you create a market in a commodity with so much supply?"

"Light is not a commodity," the Corsican said. "The same with trees and the red ant. These things are the purest of experiences. They come from the deepest verdure, from the darkness of the forest. Will you ever understand that? I trade in knowledge that purifies the knower by demonstrating the power of light over matter. Look into the pillar of light when it explodes, and you'll know what I mean."

"This is getting way too abstract for me," Wayne said. "If you want to trade in light, go for it, dude. I'm out the door, it's almost four."

"Out the door where, into another room? If you really want to get away, can I suggest Isle de Ré? It's not that far from Monsieur Maillard's Maison de Santé. You can sunburn easily there. The waters are full of electric ray-fish, but I prefer its American cousin, the electric eel. It darts when it becomes upset, stunning its prey. Look at your map of Europe and you will see the serpentine body of the eel shocking its own kind: electric power stations in London, Paris, Berlin and Rome. Electroshock. But the eel is stronger. Watch me strike at the center from the isle, the spectacle of nature destroying art."

"I'm waiting for it, nature boy."

"I feel sorry for you," the Corsican said. "You're a radical empiricist who probably thinks that Francis Bacon was a painter. Have you ever lived inside a forest? There is nothing like the itch of a red ant on your foot to make you realize the tiny sum you amount to in nature's economy."

"Fuck the red ant," Wayne said.

"If you say so," the Corsican conceded, sitting on a mound of granite overlooking the sea. "Speaking of fucking, who else have you screwed lately? This is the last piece of communication from my end. I have work to do, targets to compile."

"I'm looking forward to it," Wayne said. "Good luck, and keep me posted."

2.

THE CORSICAN WAS HAPPY to be back on the fortress island. He saw the sea as a liquid wall: a demarcation separating the island from the onslaught of modernism. He had grown accustomed to Corsica's geographic isolation, to its ninety fatal rivers, none of them navigable, to the destructive winds that wreaked havoc on its economy. There was minimal industrial activity on the island. Left behind were the carcasses of foundries, mines, mills, tanneries, the peeling façade of the

Bustaci Frères Fibre Company. He looked at the horizon. It was supposed to equilibrate life like a regulating line. Yet everything on the other side was in flux, in vertiginous gyrating motion. He did not want Corsica to become a metropolitan grid, welded together by the scaffolding of commerce.

He glanced at the shadow of the sun to determine the hour of the day. He was late for work. He turned his back to the sea to survey the elevated summits. His trusty lieutenant, Figolu, handed him an axe. He lifted it high above the liberal hand of nature toward the sky. He wondered about Wayne, whose idea of nature was Central Park. Then he came down with his axe, propelled by the force of justice, chopping off his imaginary head. The wind ripped through the air. He could hear the scratching of leaves—the sound of a haiku poem run through a paper shredder.

All around him there was bucolic disorder. The flutter of butterfly wings, the long march of the red ant, the lonely cry of the proud eagle. Branches scraped the inside of his ears, whispering to him, telling him where he should strike next, whom he should kill. There was meaning in these random noises. There was meaning in nature.

The Corsican placed the axe in a handcart. They walked for more than a day pulling the cart behind them in the direction of Corte. Before they entered the city, the Corsican stopped in front of a pine tree. He lifted the axe, pointing to the universe. His body overflowed with energy as he drove the axe deeper into the tree. He did not squander his energy; nor did he take more wood than he needed, just enough to satisfy his needs. He carefully arranged the logs in the handcart and followed the path he had taken for so many years. Each time he crossed a stream he threw in a pebble to dispel the evil spirits lurking there. He would then put his finger in the water and wet his lips as if to take communion. It was dusk when they finally reached his stone house.

"It's getting dark outside," Figolu said, chafing his hands. "Let's go in."

The Corsican walked over to the fireplace and threw a log into the *fucone.*

"I hope you're hungry. Pull up a wooden bench and make yourself at home. Dinner should be ready in a few minutes."

He sliced a *figatelli* into a cast-iron skillet; cracked three eggs along the circumference of the pan, two for him and one for Citizen Figolu, who had returned to the mountain island from the Continent to retrieve the latest sketches that Wayne had sent. Figolu sat on a bench and examined the interior of the Corsican's home. There were dusty maps here and there, books left open on benches. The walls were covered with forensic photographs of local and foreign regions facing ecological disaster. One of them depicted the rate of deforestation in the Malaysian state of Sarawak. Another described the dangers of heavy irrigation in hot, dry climates where soil had lost its virtue in the war against desertification.* With the exception of a handheld phone, there were few technological devices in the

* *Ur of the Chaldees* by Leonard Woolley.

room. There were plants of different genera positioned strategically in front of the windows. There were scattered wooden chairs and a granite table around which the commanders gathered once a week. Next to the fireplace filing cabinets contained reports on every imaginable environmental disaster in the world ever since the collapse of the Sumerian civilization. The Corsican was eager to see the contents of the sketchbook Wayne had sent, but first he asked Figolu about his observations.

In one of his first lessons during his tour of the postindustrial-scientific societies, Figolu noted that spiritual power was moving away from priests to scientists; the administration of temporal power was slowly shifting from governments to the postindustrials. There was still freedom in these secular societies, he observed, but it was subject to mediation, negotiation, compromise and consultation, so that freedom often fell victim to the tyranny of process, shrouded in technicality.

"What was it like on the other side of the horizon?"

"Chaos is present," Figolu said. "You find it on every street corner."

"It's not chaos that's present, you're confusing chaos with the spectacle," the Corsican said. "It's the spectacle that's present, on every street corner, in every household, on every screen."

The Corsican sprinkled mint leaves on the eggs and placed the skillet on the fire. "It's not easy what you do."

"You gave me good cover. *Cusi, si po franca a a morte.*" That's the way to escape death.

"Show me what you've got."

Figolu flipped open the sketchbook. It contained architectural renderings of vital structures, the regulating lines of commercial buildings rising in tiers, one behind another. They measured their dimension, length, width and angles. At the bottom of each sketch were her initials.

"Look. The Crystal Palace. This is cast iron, that's glass. It's all prefabricated material."

"I recognize it," he said.

"Mid–nineteenth century. Joseph Paxton."

"Human capacity?"

"There is no literature on that."

"Where is it?"

"Hyde Park, London."

Figolu turned the page to a drawing entitled *Chicago.*

"Recognize it?"

"Yes, she told me about it. I like the scale."

"Turn of the century. Louis Sullivan."

"What is it?"

"Department store, I think. It's the first time a metallic frame was used on the exterior of the edifice."

"Original," he said.

"If you like that, take a look at this one."

"I have no idea what it is."

"Airplane hangar at Orly. Eugène Freyssinet."

"A structural beauty."

"It's made of cement."

He turned to the middle of the sketchbook, pointing to a

drawing of a factory. "Fabrik Huttenstrasse, Berlin. Peter Behrens."

"Daunting."

"It's supposed to be the first real modernist edifice."

"The eggs are burning. Let's do this a little later."

Figolu skipped to the last page. It was a sketch of an official building resting on *pilotis* made of raw cement. The gridlike offices were equipped with a sunscreen, protecting the interior from overheating.

"This one is special. Ministry of Education. Rio de Janeiro. Oscar Niemeyer and other architects, 1937."

"Aren't you hungry?"

He flipped to another page. "Look, it's the Tokyo Stock Exchange. Yokokawa Engineering, 1988."

"It has presence."

"Except for the glass entrance."

"Glass is good," the Corsican said. "Where in Tokyo is it?"

"Two Nihonbashikabutocho, Chuo-ku."

"I'll take your word for it," he said.

Their approach was strictly objective, yet most of the drawings suffered from a poverty of execution.

"Where are these sketches coming from?" Figolu asked. "Do you recognize the initials?"

"Indeed I do," the Corsican said. "I'm sure he paid little for them."

"There is one other drawing I want you to see. It's the Pirelli Building in Milan. Gio Ponti. It's the last word in elegance."

"You're a saint."

"A hungry saint."

"The eggs are burnt."

They considered another drawing. The Corsican was intoxicated by the structures, drowned in the details of scale and dimension.

"This one looks like an airport."

"It's Gatwick. York, Rosenberg and Masdall, 1958."

"She may have mentioned it to me."

"I always wanted to be an architect," Figolu said.

"You are, a fallen architect, an architect of death."

Figolu did not take this comment well, for it was a comparison to the funereal architecture of the fascists, whose monumental and classicist visions he abhorred. A studious and unassuming man, he spent his younger years inside a tree house in the Valley of Restonica until the Corsican anointed him ambassador to the world. His transformation from recluse to world traveler was not entirely unnatural, for Figolu came from a family with a proud military tradition. "*Sans la Corse et les Corses pas de colonization Française,*" affirmed his grandfather, the great General Gouraudi.

"I could never be an architect of death," he said finally. "I still have my beliefs."

"Don't be upset, my dear Figolu. Come, let's eat."

And it was true, they did have their beliefs, warped as they may have been by the internal contradictions of their individual and collective circumstances. They went everywhere in defense of nature: its prickly stems, its bramble and bush, its plundered chronometric cycles, its crippled calendar, the coded tapestry of its patterns, the singular and undeviating beauty of its hills, standing stubbornly in the way of human progress.

In the month that followed, many buildings fell. The first was the vaunted Tokyo Stock Exchange. A week later the Crystal Palace* came crashing down. Then a Range Rover rigged with explosives destroyed a section of the Fabrik Huttenstrasse. A survivor was quoted on German television as saying, "Everything has its end, only the sausage has two." Despite his good-natured fatalism, the man was clearly out of breath. It was useless to treat tragedy with humor when faced with the absoluteness of death. The coup de grâce was the Ministry of Education in Rio. Its edifice was graciously spared, but not its personnel. They perished in less than an hour as a serpentine, jaundiced fume billowed its way through the building's ventilation system. Upon hearing the news, Rio descended into collective delirium.

The Corsican and his commanders gathered in his home to take stock of events. "Nature has struck back," Figolu said, "and it will strike again."

* The Crystal Palace in London was actually destroyed by fire in 1882.

As a sign of the rising stakes, the mountain island reinforced its security. Solar-powered jeeps roamed Corte's parameter with characteristic impunity. They had nicknames like "Pristine" and "Pozzo de Borgo" stenciled on their sides. At the time, the autonomous units were busy carrying a flurry of operational instructions from the center to the coast. They smuggled the letters on fishing ships destined for the terrestrial units on the Continent.

As head of operations, Figolu provided a geographic summary of their performance to date.

"In the northern hemisphere, where law enforcement agencies are on full alert, we are generally meeting high resistance with a success rate that is lower than what we are aiming for," he said. "Given room for operational improvement, we hope to achieve levels of chaos that are more in line with our European record."

"Does this mean that the mix of operations is now more heavily weighted toward Europe?" asked one of the commanders.

"Well, let me say that European integration has resulted in porous borders all across the Continent and that we have been a beneficiary of this. We are seeing relatively easy cross-border movements in Europe and this has certainly been a positive contributing factor to our overall performance there."

One of the commanders wondered what had gotten into Figolu. When had he started to speak this way? In his memory, Figolu was a teenager perched in a tree house. Little Figolu.

How times had changed. And now, as the organization grew, its leaders sounded more and more like those on the Continent, like people who had lost their native insouciance in the uncompromising pursuit of power.

"What are you seeing in the Asian markets?" asked another commander. "Can you comment on the possibility of outsourcing and what impact, if any, this could have on reducing our overhead?"

"Well, let me take your second question first," Figolu said. "It's too early to tell the impact on overhead, but we are exploring the possibility of working with outside groups. We all know the advantages of a horizontally structured organization on the SG&A line. As far as Asia and the Subcontinent are concerned, we are still weighing our options, thinking very carefully about how to restore chaos there. Clearly, the Tokyo big bang has touched a raw nerve in the region, with its expected and expectant effects being felt everywhere in ripple-like fashion. Tokyo was our big earthquake, the event that has put the rest of the Continent on standby."

"Thank you, Fig," the Corsican said. "Can you now give us an overview of the financials?"

"Well, our balance sheet remains robust. Payables have shrunk for the third consecutive quarter. Cash reserves are at their highest historic levels following a significant capital injection from an offshore fund."

"Fig, any special situations we need to be aware of?"

"There is one noteworthy mention. We have entered into a

special arrangement with this offshore fund I mentioned. We are now symbiotically connected to the *spectacle.*"

"Thank you, Fig. That concludes the conference; you may now disconnect."

3.

THE FOLLOWING WEEK the Corsican hosted a spectacle on the theme of nature as a counter-ideal to technology. Thousands of ecologists gathered at the center of the island to hear him speak. The Valley of Restonica was packed with camping gear, tiki torches and tribal flags adorned with environmental symbols. The summit had wide representation. There were the Naturalists, who were naturally promoting the protection of migratory birds. There were the Situationists, who were eager to present their draft proposal for a New International Economic situation. There were the Brazilians, who wanted to learn about the secure land use rights for traditional forest dwellers in the Amazon Basin and who also just wanted to party. Together, they made up a loose interconnection of environmental groups that worked together on various campaigns to defend nature. But there were also underground cells that worked in complete autonomy, disabling units that operated in the deepest of the metropolis. One of their leaders had vandalized the home of a famous chef, known for his foie gras, to protest the force-feeding of geese. Another had launched a rocket-propelled grenade into a Dutch freezer ship at the edge of the continental shelf. They came to the mountain island to hear the opening remarks of the Corsican on the state of nature and the final war against technological innovation.

The Valley of Restonica was shrouded in a cool milky haze. The sky was steel gray, a shade darker than the crowded steps of Rue Scoliscia. The faithful numbered in the thousands, waiting for the Corsican to speak. Streams of human flesh poured out of the valley and marched into Corte. Many of them were forced into adjacent side streets around a public square. A teenager in camouflage climbed the statue of General Gafforj, standing on the plinth for a better view of the speaker. A poster of the Corsican fluttered proudly from the general's sword. The Corsican finally emerged from the barrack into the citadel. The spectators remained silent, raising their fists. They faded into each other in all sorts of combinations and permutations, so that the crowd swelled into a mixture of disjointed beliefs joined together by a common desire.

The Corsican walked down the steps of the citadel toward the square. There was nothing grandiose or gilded about the square. Its composition was austere and essential. When he reached the podium he did not bother to wave at the crowd.

There was little time to waste, for after his speech he had to make arrangements for his meeting with Wayne.

"The Industrial Revolution and its consequences have failed the human race," he said, addressing the faithful. "They have greatly increased the life expectancy of those who live in advanced countries, but they have destabilized and fragmented society. They have made life unfulfilling. They have subjected human beings to indignities. They have led to widespread psychological suffering, and they have inflicted severe damage on the natural world. The continued development of technology will only exasperate this situation."

Hearing these words, the crowd broke into thunderous applause. Many waved candles in the air, which from a distance looked like white prairie fires. The Corsican continued, "The industrial-technological system may survive, or it may break down. If it survives, it may eventually achieve a low level of physical and psychological suffering, but only after passing through a long and very painful period of adjustment."*

The Corsican stared into the crowd with his strange protuberant eyes. His thoughts were strewn across multiple time zones. He thought about New York. It was a matter of operational consequence that an apartment building in Manhattan contained more people than a traditional neighborhood. He considered the geometric model of traffic flow exemplified in Haussmann's great plan of the Grands Boulevards; the nodes of

* Excerpts from Ted Kaczynski.

access that led to the Concorde. He was determined to de-Haussmannize Paris one day, to turn the City of Light into a City of Darkness. What fueled his anger? Was it the surging price of oil at $50 a barrel? Was it because he was fired from the Bustaci Frères Fibre Company? Whatever it was, he would strike soon. It was only a matter of time, of which there seemed to be plenty in Corsica.

He concluded:

"As Citizen Jean-Jacques Rousseau observed, civilized man is a perverse beast. The civil societies he has constructed are bankrupt, their scientific foundations hopelessly spurious."

There was silence, then came the triumphant cry of an endangered eagle.

The Accidental Architect

1.

In one of his last emails Wayne had asked Alix for a detailed sketch of the cement structure that housed the Tokyo Stock Exchange, in addition to drawings of the Crystal Palace in London. With each passing day he sent her more technical questions. She was happy to answer them, not the least because his requests put her in a position to showcase her talents. It was with this excessive optimism that she walked back home and adjusted the volume of her portable music player. An infectious rhythm spread from a tiny device strapped to her waist through her body:

*Aux sang chaud s'agitent sublime, sordide l'exaltation . . ."**

* Jihane.

The streets were empty in anticipation of booming thunder, except for a homeless man who pushed a shopping cart in her direction. At first she mistook him for a halal hot dog vendor, but this was a simulacrum, a transplanted image from her trip to Manhattan. She walked past him and stopped in front of a shop called Madame Zaza of Marseille. She peered into the window display. There was a yellow top she admired, a black skirt by Ange Paris. She went inside and tried them on. When she stepped out, the clouds rumbled. She ran for cover in the lobby of a nearby building. She took the elevator up to the roof. When the doors opened she ran to the edge of the building. She was propelled by a pulsating hip-hop beat. She sprinted from one end of the roof to the other, submerged in her own fulminating thunder, the source of which even she did not know. *La criture est une violence. La criture est directe. La criture est une gerbe. Une gerbe est un jet direct. La criture est un jet de simplicité. La criture est violente. Elle envoie un jet de matière simple. La criture est violente. La beauté est simple.**

* *Criture* is writing without the letter *w*. *Une gerbe* is a bouquet of flowers, yet it also means vomit. Excerpt from Arno.

2.

In the aftermath of the Tokyo bombing, the Industrial Bank of Japan and many other city banks nervously watched their asset prices fizzle. Selling spread like the plague. Within a few months, the Nikkei lost a staggering 28 percent of its market value. The CAC 40 shed 23 percent. The tech-laden Nasdaq fell 26 percent. The London Stock Exchange dropped 21 percent. Fortunately for Wayne, the future was in the past; a week before the implosion he received a coded message from the Corsican: "There will no longer be a *raven* in the space-time region of Tokyo. The building will have to go."

If Wayne was quickest to react to the news, equity analysts were the slowest. Many weeks passed before they warned investors of a global deflationary spiral. The stream of bad news had no end in sight. Brazil announced a moratorium on its external debt obligations. The Belgian central bank business confidence index plunged to a historic low. And then, as if all of this were not trouble enough, the charismatic dean of the Grand Mosque of Paris, Sheikh Tariq Mashkal, issued a pronouncement that the hamburger was no longer culturally neutral:

"We will boycott them, the Pepsi and the Coca-Cola and the McDonald burger," he said. "This is forbidden, the Kentucky chicken and the McDonald burger. Why should we allow from abroad these things? I appeal to the conscience of the *ummah.* Will you consider buying instead a can of Mecca-Cola?"

The eye of the financial storm, however, remained in Japan. The vicious unwinding of the financial system decimated hundreds of companies on the Tokyo Stock Exchange. Encouraged by this bleak cascade of news, Wayne tilted his portfolio in favor of a systemic failure of the future.

Chaos, of course, was hardly spontaneous. It required research and development. When a leading benchmark fell more than two percent, Wayne looked for correlation. His head was a repository of all that was dreadful in the world: significant dates and political events in financial market history that he organized according to a system of numeric notation only he could decode. It was a heavy workload. He mastered the science of mnemonics so that he memorized crop conditions from seventy years ago. But did he remember what the market did the day his first cousin Wilfred got married, or the day his economics professor sent him a congratulatory email, or the day he refused to help his neighbor put up a Christmas tree because he had an e-meeting with an alternative energy company on the Digital Coast?

No way, dude.

Wayne walked over to the office kitchen in search of a cool Cherry Coke. The intern had taken the last can, the little shit. He grabbed a warm carton of orange juice from the counter.

Morning without Tropicana Pure Premium? Not an option.

It was Armageddon outside and he needed all the vitamin

C Tropicana could offer. He took a sip, feeling more tired than ever. In a nanosecond of happiness he recalled the very first day he emailed Alix. Hours later, as he left the office, he bumped into a homeless man with a scraggly beard. The man held him from his shoulders and politely asked for twenty dollars. What chutzpah, Wayne thought. He reached into his pocket and pulled out a hundred. He did not share this incident with anyone. So much of history is unwritten, a lost continuum of unspoken moments, a contradiction to all that has been said about him: trader without a heart, rapacious swindler, penny-pinching predator, timorous scumbag, murderer. Rumors. Do not believe them. They are there to be denied, or, if the market is open, to be traded on.

IT WAS LUNCHTIME AT Empiricus Kapital. Dr. Wang placed two brown bags on the conference table. He thought about offering a lollipop to Polly, the well-endowed office administrator with whom he wanted to establish a level of proximity. The secretary with big wapiti eyes spurned most of his advances. She preferred to spend her nights reading Murakami novels. The rest of the Empiricus staff remained glued to their spreadsheets, always with a predilection for identifying error. Banerjee, the chief research analyst, considered the widening spread between emerging market bonds and U.S. Treasuries, trying to discern the makings of a potential political crisis. Next to him sat Cordoba. She composed an email to a colleague at

Santander Bank, explaining why purchasing power parity was a poor tool for currency forecasting.

"Hey Brainiac," she wrote, "don't forget. Because of different national tastes and preferences, countries may weight the goods and services that comprise their price baskets differently. So you end up comparing apples to oranges. You're mixing your fruits, Pablo."

As for Dr. Wang, he was busy changing the background music from Erik Satie to Arvo Pärt because the Baltic composer was better suited to volatility. Such an exalted level of intellectual activity. If they only knew of the compromises he made in the service of expediency. Wayne entered the conference room and emptied the contents of the brown bags: an egg-white omelet and Diet Coke for the secretary, ham on rye for Banerjee, crab cakes and mashed potatoes for Cordoba, chicken curry for Dr. Wang, an avocado sandwich with sun-dried tomatoes for himself, absolutely nothing for the intern, the little shit. Let him go to McDonald's across the street. Supersize him. Wayne grabbed his sandwich and walked back to his desk. He pulled out the tattered copy of *Capital* from his drawer and read the preface by Frederick Engels:

> *On the 14th of March, at a quarter to three in the afternoon, the greatest living thinker ceased to think. The gap that has been left by the departure of this mighty spirit will soon enough make itself felt. Just as Darwin discovered the law of development of organic nature, so Marx discovered*

> *the law of development of human history: The simple fact, hitherto concealed by an outgrowth of ideology, that mankind must first of all have shelter and clothing, eat and drink. . . .*

Wayne bit into his avocado sandwich. He felt a presentiment. As with a mountaineer moving from a fixed point to its consequence, below him stood an empty space. What would happen if the cord broke and he fell into an abyss, into another time zone many continents away? A land free of substitute objects, of dead passions, where the next best thing was more than a nothing, and the valiant vascular organ that was the heart, the essential, incandescent future. He traced the trajectory of his life from the time of his adolescence to the present. When he was young he had wanted to be a teacher. Then at the age of twenty he met Elizabeth in college. Everything had become temporary, like the flickering symbols on his screen. It was exciting to hold on to a stock for two weeks, then dump it. At twenty-seven he felt fluid. Like stateless, protean capital he went to where he was wanted and stayed where he was treated well. If the host asked him to leave, it was not before he pissed on the floor. Then one day he opened his first trading account at Datek.

He stared at the Bloomberg. His eyes were empty electrical sockets. He was breathing heavily now, ready to bet on the next disaster. A real-time headline scrolled up the screen, then another, then another. There was an explosion along the

Mediterranean basin. It was a sinking cruise liner and on board were several billionaires. Ship ahoy, Wayne thought, fucking maggots. The American Stock Exchange was still closed. All around the world thousands of traders read the same news from competing data providers about the sinking ship with the executives on board. A global electronic plebiscite would take place soon on whether to buy stocks or sell them. At the bell, stocks surged. The European exchanges erupted violently in the direction of the heavens. It was unreal, spectacular.

Wayne stared at his screen in disbelief. In the week that followed, the market stormed higher against Empiricus Kapital; the fund posted losses day after day. "This is insane," Wayne said. "All the talking heads are bullin' this thing up. Yesterday, the Middle East was getting ass-fucked. Today, everyone is in love. I don't get it."

It would not be long before the U.S. government released a flurry of statistics confirming the economic expansion. Sales of single-family homes rocketed to a seasonally adjusted high. The semiconductor industry book-to-bill ratio rose 1.7 percent. Corporate profits recovered, with many companies regaining something called "pricing power," the capitalist's approving euphemism for benign inflation. Wayne felt nauseous. Most of this information was error-prone and manipulated anyway. He held on to his positions, convinced that the market would resume its downward spiral. He stuck six yellow Post-its on Simone Cordoba's Bloomberg screens:

Hey genius, fasten your seat belt. We managed to give back in just a few weeks all of the gains we achieved in the last six months. The months ahead will require fortitude and patience. I want you to keep especially alert, looking for opportunities on the downside as we enter a period of heightened political and economic uncertainty; much grist for the worry mill . . .

Hold still.

$$$ Wayne.

3.

As the historical trade-off between aggregate supply and demand broke down, so did Wayne. A number of indicators confirmed the sustainability of the expansion. Brent Crude oil pulled back. Alternative fuel adoption rates soared. The expected rate of inflation subsided. So did unemployment. It was yet another blow to the Phillips curve. He turned to his trusty Bloomberg. All that he could see was the reflection of his desperate face, a pathetic knowledge worker falling behind events. There was a blank interiorized gleam in his eyes. He stared at his pampered hands, poised on an ergonomic keyboard. He pretended he was Rachmaninoff playing a mournful prelude, an end-of-the-world elegy to humanity. His fingers trembled. He took an uncertain sip of coffee. He read the cheerful headlines on his computer screen. It made him sick. It was as though happiness had been universally engineered, permanently planted into people's DNA like a company trust mark: Spectacle Inside, Outside, On Every Side. Happiness Everywhere, in every time zone and handheld device.

It took less than a week for the world to become safe. The Middle East moved closer to a permanent, lasting peace. The number of seasonally adjusted bombing victims in Abidjan posted a year-over-year decline. The civil unrest participation rate in Africa fell. The cross-price elasticity of demand for grenades and rocket launchers also fell. After endless leads and lags, Iran gave up its nuclear ambitions. This was unbidden, unwelcome news for Wayne. He suddenly felt uncomfortable in his chair, custom designed for the digital derrière. He accessed the Internet. He browsed. Bought a book. Went back to work. A few more keystrokes followed, a few more gulps of coffee, and he launched a powerful intuitive application. It was supposed to help him compare the level of investor fear in different markets.

But there was no fear.

The good old days were back again. At least that was what the headlines said. Religions no longer split us. Politics no longer polarized us. Incompatible technologies no longer came between us.

Everywhere he looked, companies engaged in spectacular promotion. Some executives backdated their options to price them at a lower level. As the founder of one venture capital firm put it, "When an economy grows, everyone is happy. Investors lose their interest in *detaily* stuff, they become more *concepty.* It's sort of like falling in love: the impossible becomes possible."

And so investors fell in love with the market again. Wayne paled at the implications. He remained the prodigal evangelist of doom, Wall Street's chief dissident. He scoured the Bloomberg for headlines from only days before when the world was still a precarious place: "Tutsi Refugees Fear Fresh Massacres by Hutus," "Battling the AIDS Pandemic: the Subcontinent at a Crossroads," "Violence-Racked Pakistan Becoming a New Crisis for U.S.," "Chemical Factory Explosion Leaves Thirty Dead."

The world had reinvented itself in a week.

Somehow the economy had entered into a self-sustaining recovery and billions of dollars poured into stock funds. Whether this was reality or a refraction of reality, the practical pitfalls for Empiricus remained the same. Wayne needed another crisis to derail the market. He picked up his handheld and left a message for the Corsican:

"I have several *buy-side* mandates looking for potential targets," he said.

A week later he received a postcard at his Tribeca loft. At first he thought it was from Alix. He examined the photo with anticipation. There was an idyllic portrait of a citadel perched on a white calciferous cliff overlooking the sea. Strange-shaped *calanques* jutted out of the raging water. A seagull flew over the Piazza di Manichila. Wayne wondered what it would be like to live in Bonifacio, to hear the howl of the *libeccio.* The only foreign winds he knew were confined to the atlas, tempestuous twisters, jetstreams, the Kuroshio Current, the hot, dusty *khamsin* reduced to the calm coordinates of fine print in twelve-point Palatino typeface—the gust pulled out of them. He turned the postcard around and began to read:

"We have your instructions but I am running low on reserves. We need more success fees before signing and closing. Otherwise, weather good here. Fish is to die for. Can you confirm our meeting in Marseille?"

Wayne left another message on his voice mail: "You know what they say, that a slow deal is a dead deal. I want you to strike like lightning and this time put in some leverage. See you a week from today. I will be staying at the Unité."

The next day, Gordon Brown, the Chancellor of the Exchequer, exploded on the staid steps of the Bank of England. In a staggering operation—executed with both deterministic certitude and fatalistic splendor—a suicide bomber with a rudimentary device strapped to his belly walked up to Mr. Brown and gave him a bear hug. First came the blast, followed by a warm gust of body parts and debris, confusion compressed, reality tangled, unraveled, reordered. This was followed by a spectacular silence, then panic flooded the city, sirens and lamentations. And after a while Mr. Brown's corporal remains were televised on many networks and in many time zones: full-frontal entertainment for a shock-averse world. Indeed, the currency markets hardly flinched. The dignified pound, undeterred, stood firm on the day of the assassination, trading at a lofty level. Wayne's planned bet of a sterling meltdown did not come to pass, a reminder that the universe was not a mathematical conglomerate of unified coordinates.

He had to do something, quickly, to change the course of the sterling's direction. He emailed Seth Santorini at the Quantum Fund. But there was a transmission error in the packet-switching network and the message never reached its destination. It traveled back through a carnival of wires, loops and switches to his inbox. He looked at his watch. It was six p.m. in Silicon Alley, three p.m. on the Digital Coast, almost midnight in Marseille. He left another message for Seth, this time on his voice mail: "Hey Dickwad, it's me. I'm not sure if you have a position in this fucking piece of shit, but if you do, hold on. This motherfucking gravy train is on its last run."

4.

FOR THE FIRST TIME in months the train ran on time. Alix took a seat next to the window, destination unknown. The train swirled past a patch of pine in the direction of l'Estaque, where fishermen wrestled with twitching mullet on the boardwalk. When the train made its stop she got off and walked down to the dilapidated quay. It was a bright and sunny day. There were earth-baked pots at the entrance, home to red and white tulips, their lance-shaped petals in bloom. There was no sign of gloom. She strolled along the periphery of the harbor, then stepped into a bar to take stock of the changing times; to toast the rehabilitation of the metropolis, the lifting of the Green Line, the restitution of the fish market at the Vieux Port, the sun-drenched quay. She was dressed for the occasion too, a pretty girl in sandals, playing the part of an ingénue. She wore a miniskirt, wool silk mix, twill weave. It barely covered the lower precincts of her bottom. She felt exposed, desired. She returned to the station, took the train along the coast past sun-hammered inlets. It was the first time that she had seen the Mediterranean axis in more than a year, an endless expanse of shimmering blue and gold. The train burrowed through tunnels, past gorges and ravines, gnarled and fissured rock. It stopped at Martigues.

The city was an outcrop of petrochemical refineries and Baroque chapels, quaint quays and cranes, soot-stained bridges and pastel-colored buildings, an unlikely mosaic of mutual coexistence. She got off the train and walked to the city hall, an art deco composite of checkered blue and white. She entered the building and went up to the roof. The mistral was nowhere to be found and the smell of petrol had sunk into town. She walked to the edge of the building. Beyond the quays was an industrial landscape that was home to two BP-Amoco and TotalFinaElf refineries. She took a deep breath. A whiff of benzene rushed into her nose. There was a crane in the not-so-far distance that had begun to scratch the surface of what's possible. It was great to be alive, in spite of, perhaps because of, the Industrial Revolution. And there was another revolution—a more septic one—that empowered users across an entirely new range of portable devices, giving them access to information from any place in the world. And it wasn't just access to information. It was the power to visit new worlds, to see everything and to be heard everywhere. Those little portable boxes and tiny screens transmitted the avarice, the jealousy, the loneliness, the love and inspiration manifest in humanity. They organized her weekends, her idle days, her furtive sex life. Her libido shot up every time her mobile buzzed. This time it was a *texto* from Wayne:

"See you soon," he wrote. "I send you all my love in infrared bitstreams."

Made in Marseille

1.

THE NINE-STORY BUILDING stood on thirty triangular pillars. Each measured eight meters high. It was a futuristic machine, an industrial block of tangled wires, pipes and progress tucked behind a flesh of raw cement. Its exterior was oppressive, absent of any ornament. Behind the walls were its vital systems, jammed into tight little metal conduits.

Wayne stepped out of the taxi and set his suitcase down. He marveled at the structural virtuosity of the building. His head swirled, an inverted vertigo in his mind. There was a breeze, a slight rustle from the surrounding trees. His knees buckled, not so much at the power of nature, but at the power of man's experimental art. He felt nature in retreat, on the run. The wind crawled back into the crevices of the surrounding hills. It was dusk. There was no trace of the sun. He walked to the entrance of the building. A silver plaque next to the glass doors read:

THE PURPOSE OF THIS BUILDING IS
TO GIVE TO THE MEN OF THE SECOND
MACHINE CIVILIZATION A NEW HOME.

Inside, there was a hotel, 337 apartments, a preschool, a bakery and a gym. He remembered the explosion at the Tokyo Stock Exchange. The velocity of bodies falling down by the pull of gravity was independent of their weight.

The first time he saw the building he felt that he was in the middle of an industrial park. He was surrounded by the certainty of cement, standing in the dark. He stood underneath the building, stretching out his arms between two pillars. They were supposed to be the fructifying blossoms of nature itself. He wanted to pluck them one by one. He took the elevator up to the hotel on the third floor. When the doors opened, Alix was waiting for him. He tugged her softly toward him. For the next two days he saw very little of Marseille. They took their breakfast on the rooftop terrace, dined at the hotel restaurant. At night she read Guy Debord under the bed lamp as he kissed her loins.

"Kiss me," she said. Like the sea, her legs stretched out, then retracted. She put her book down and began to moan, a moan that turned into a cry without tears.

"Come up," she said. "Quickly."

When they made love he felt as though he were swimming, until she billowed into a frothing wave, lifting him with her hips, then crashing into him. Sometimes he took her from behind. He would press her back down, the bending resistance of her spine, into the wrinkled bedsheets. During these moments of coital contact, their bodies moved like a wave, as if the building itself were billowing, a seismic orgasm that crashed in the face of reason. When they lay on the sheets he imagined the floors collapsing, like a stack of pancakes, hurling flying embers, ash, rubble and twisted steel.

One morning they decided to leave the building. They put their sneakers on and boarded bus #21 to the outskirts of Marseille.

"We'll get off at the last stop, near my architecture school," she said. "It's the start of the hiking trail."

"I forgot my handheld in the room," he said.

"Good," she said. "Hold my hand instead. Did you take the *coppa* and the bread?"

"I took the *coppa,*" he said. "We don't have bread. I took what I could."

He looked around him. It was the first time in a long while that he had contemplated nature. The jagged, serrated hills were covered in mist. He was overtaken by a most unnatural urge. He wanted to hug a tree. As they descended into the valley he saw a steely lizard dart out of a bush. Then a toad leapt in front of him. He had never seen a toad outside of his high school science class. He wondered what other amphibians were hiding in the grass. He lost himself in the perpetual patch of green. He considered throwing his handheld electronic organizer into a ravine: the seedling of a microchip decomposed into the detritus of the earth to give birth to a lofty tree with little Palm Pilots hanging from its digital branches. They walked along a winding dirt path through an eclectic variety of insects and plants. They drank from the cold, crystalline water of a stream. They followed an overgrown trail down a steep slope that led to a cove. He forgot where he was until the cry of an eagle pierced the unbroken silence around them. They sat down next to a lizard and ate the *coppa,* the diaphanous slices of Italian charcuterie through which he could see the orange, iridescent sun. He was about to devour another slice when she reached out and touched him.

"I want to see your *fauve,*" she said.

"My what?"

"Your *fauve.*"

She ran her fingers through his fur.

"There's no one around, except for the lizard. Show it to me."

The lizard lashed out its libidinous tongue. *Listen to her,* it seemed to say. *It's not an unreasonable request.* He unbuttoned his pants. She touched him, the hand of beneficent nature caressing his sex.

"I want to be his friend," she said.

His emotions vibrated at a frequency of several kilohertz per second, technology never too far behind the cycles of nature. There was something strange happening to him. He knew that there was more to these inchoate sexual stirrings than just sex itself. Yet he did not know what was at stake, which side to take.

"What does it look like, my *fauve*?" he asked.

"It has a tired, nonchalant beauty," she said. "Watch me change that."

He had never been so open to change. She held his fingers and guided them to the back of her jeans. She took a deep breath. A whiff of pine-scented air rushed into her nose.

"A little higher," she said. "A little lower. Now squeeze my bottom."

2.

THE FOLLOWING NIGHT she took him to the bourgeois-bohem neighborhood of Cours Julien.

"A lot of artists live here. It's our Williamsburg, but the rents are cheaper."

"It's a demanding profession," he said. "Unless if you're a Jasper Johns and you can sell a drawing of the American flag for one million dollars."

"Be more polite," she said.

They made their way to Bar du Champs and ordered a pint of beer. Next to them was an unemployed poet in a Peruvian bonnet reading yesterday's copy of *L'Humanité.* They quaffed down their beer and walked back to the courtyard, past a giant clay pot full of tulips. Wayne tore off a red lance-shaped petal and offered it to Alix. On the window ledge of a nearby building were zinc tubs and glass receptacles marked by profuse and delicate ornamentation. The city beamed with bushels of bougainvillea, sunflowers and dandelions. Other subtle changes took place outside of the metropolis. In the latest edition of her dictionary reality was once again being reorganized. A number of gloomy words like *anxiosphère* were left out. New ones made their way in. Few people knew the editors who made these important decisions. Yet there was a growing consensus that their collective wisdom augured a brighter, kinder future. And it was not just words. There was practical, material, empirical, experiential, quantifiable, scientific, spectacular evidence that the forces of order were making a comeback in the world.

As recently as yesterday, city officials announced plans to expand the metro network to link the outlying districts of the north with the wealthy ones along the coast. From Malmousk to Les Goudes, the the coastal highway gave way to a blissful indolence. Wayne too walked to the lazy rhythm of the sea. If his steps were slow, it was not because he was weighed down by the gravity of his sins, but by the panoply of his portable devices: his trusty BlackBerry, satellite phone and Palm Pilot.

They approached the water fountain at the center of Cours Julien. Alix made a wish and threw the tulip petal into the water.

"Now it's your turn."

Wayne reached into his pocket and grabbed a euro coin.

"No, no," she said. "Something else."

"Like what?"

"Like one of your phones."

She pointed to the BlackBerry.

"That's not a phone. It's a BlackBerry."

"Whatever. Throw it in the water."

"But it's my lifeline to the world."

"Throw. It. In. The. Wa-ter."

"You don't even know what you're saying."

"Throw it in the water. Go with your instinct."

"But what do I get in return?"

"Not everything is a trade."

"Most everything is a trade."

She kissed his temple.

"That's not a trade."

"That's worth a million dollars."

"I won't take it. You can keep it."

"Maybe."

"That's good."

"What's good?"

"You said maybe. That's good."

"So what are you asking me?"

"To throw your Berryblack in the water. I'm not sure what I am asking you. I think you already know what I'm asking you."

He made a wish. He reached for the BlackBerry and threw

it into the water. It was the death of at least one microchip, the size of a thumbnail, containing as much as a quarter mile of infinitesimal wires, sinking into the murky water.

They made their way around the fountain to Le Jardin d'Acôté, one of the many restaurants in the courtyard. Before they walked in, Wayne saw a man contentedly pissing against the wall.

"I like it here," he said. "It doesn't look too expensive."

"If you prefer North African, I know of another place."

Wayne shook his head. Couscous did not have a high place in his affections.

"What about this?" she asked, and kissed his temple softly. "How much is that worth to you?"

When they entered the restaurant a blackout struck the metropolis. In the temperate zones along the Mediterranean many electrical power stations failed. Wayne stretched out his arm and held her hand. More than one molecule of sentiment awakened in him. She could barely make out his outline in the porous darkness, until specks of candlelight descended between them. She noticed that his cheeks had turned red. He spotted a firefly on her plate, a nocturnal lightning bug that produced its own internal lamp. She searched for the firefly's companion and was relieved to find her on the night window, emitting bright throbs from the luminescent chemicals in her abdominal organs.

"Look," he said. "There are two of them."

"Let's eat quickly and get back to the hotel, but I have to go somewhere first. I promised to meet a friend at the port for a drink."

"Don't let her kidnap you," Wayne said. "Come back."

"I won't be long."

"I have a short meeting too, shouldn't take long. Come up to my room when you're done."

"Okay," she said. "Hey, look at the fireflies. They've landed between us; one of them is eating our bread."

When dinner arrived, they both went through it with procedural alacrity. She did not finish her goat cheese. He looked bored with his dried mullet eggs. He paid the bill, and for once did not upset the waitress by failing to leave a tip. They walked down Rue d'Aubagne and he took a taxi back to the hotel, but when he got there the Corsican was not there. He asked the doorman if there were any messages for him. There were none. He walked back out and circled the building twice and there was no sign of him. The Corsican was now fifteen minutes late. He looked up to the building and wondered if he should go up to his room to get the money, equally divided between dollar, euro and yen. Most of the balconies were pitch-black. Then in the distance he saw a cab move next to the curb and someone stepped out into the darkness. He could not make out who it was. Moments later the figure waved and sprinted in his direction. As she came closer, Wayne realized that it was Alix. She threw herself into him and they fell down.

"I changed my mind," she said. "I didn't want to see him."

"I see," Wayne said. "So your friend was a man?"

"It's not important, and how was your meeting?"

"It doesn't look like it's going to happen. We'll have to reschedule."

"Come on, let's run around the columns." She jumped to her feet.

They weaved in and out of the triangular pillars, which were made of cement, yet looked organic, as if they had grown from the earth. They walked into the lobby and said good night to the doorman, who had just switched on the backup generators. In the elevator, Wayne tenaciously clung to her hand as they went up to the roof; she asked him what wish he had made when he threw his BlackBerry into the fountain. He wanted them to go to Corsica one day, where he had a friend who resembled the human reincarnation of a sublime species of fish, condemned by some supernatural power to live among ordinary men. He had strange protuberant eyes and chewed on flower petals. He would give them an idyllic tour of the mountain island. He would take them into a forest in search of chestnuts. He would shelter them in the rugged mountains of Corte, from the unbearable noise of the postindustrial world, the pell-mell of commerce, the constant churning of dollars and euros and yen and coins and keys to access rooms and anterooms, safes and vaults and filing cabinets and drawers and secret compartments that led to other secret compartments. He wished that he had no keys or keywords, that he was a shepherd in a vast amber field. He would tend to the woolly sheep, cane in hand, laptop in his briefcase, just in case.

"That's more than one wish," she said. "Anyway, I don't want to go to Corsica. We have everything here."

"What was yours?"

"You'll see."

When the elevator doors opened, she bounced into the darkness. He thought he had lost her. He took several steps into the night. She was now behind Wayne. She approached him from the back and wrapped her arms around him. They walked to the edge of the roof. The city was black, enshrouded in volcanic glass. As they walked along the edge of the building, they heard the wind howl: the sound of a haiku poem run through a paper shredder. She knew the power of this wind, how it could transform vast oceans into ancient dust, Anatolian desert. He felt the tenebrous warmth of her body against his, her hand reaching down into his pants. They came down to their knees, touching the cold cement.

"Do you want to know my wish?"

"What is it?"

"First you take off everything."

Moments later he lost his head in the swollen diadem of her body. She pulled her knees back.

"Come here," she said.

He was about to when they heard a rumbling noise that grew into rolling thunder. There was a scurry on the stairwell, followed by a scream. He did not pay attention to it, planting his hands flat against the cement, thrusting his kidneys into her. Then he heard a loud metallic noise and a snap.

"What is it?" she said.

"I don't know."

"Keep going."

He thought he saw a blue flash, a vivid orange flame that sprang from the surrounding darkness. It changed color, then burst into an exploding pillar of light. He was spellbound.

"Did you see the flash?"

"Come back here."

"What did you wish for?"

"For you to find the disaster of your taste," she said. "Hey, don't look so serious, I'm just joking."

3.

WHEN THE CORSICAN heard the explosion, he thought that it was the culmination of the perfect spectacle. But then he looked at his watch and saw that there was no one else around him. He stood up on the steps of the hotel. He was unable to move and slowly tears filled his eyes. And while in Wayne's eyes there was fear and confusion, he spoke with the highest conviction. It was then that the columns buckled and the roof lost its support, leaving it precariously exposed. Throughout the building hundreds of bolts failed. Their bodies conjoined in a seismic jolt, destabilized by a lateral pull.

"I love you too" were her last words before they were sucked into a black vacuum, into the falling debris, into what was once a phantasmagorical living machine, having lost all measure and proportion. The explosion tore the façade from the building, hurling flying embers, chunks of cement and conical footings, yet somehow Wayne and Alix remained intertwined even as they fell through the lower floors in rapid sequence. When the dust settled, entombed in the rubble were many bodies, but only theirs was one, like the twisted girders of progress around them, or a poignant still life worthy of a Sotheby's auction.

If Wayne were alive, surely he would have paid ten million dollars for it.

Acknowledgments

I would like to thank Melanie Jackson, Sarah Hochman and Geoff Kloske, Jason and Jeremy, Buster and Justyna, J. Merriwether and A. Garibaldi, Troy and Jatin, Warren and Pegor, Atom and Olivier, Nancy and Ehud, Wayne and Charlotte, Nassim and Laura, Greg B., and James D., and my family.

About the Author

Viken Berberian is the author of the novel *The Cyclist.* His work has appeared in *The New York Times,* the *Los Angeles Times* and the *Financial Times.* He lives in Manhattan, Marseille and Paris.